What Others Litchfield Writ

MW01600408

In such a fast-paced world, it is a pleasure to be able to slow down and grab a piece of reality. The Litchfield Writer's Group has given me such a break.
-- Bob Greenhow, Owner KLFD AM1410 Litchfield

Just like coming home... the talent in our own community is so inspiring.
-- Nicole Johnson, Proprietress, Nicola's Coffee and More, Litchfield

Tapping into local talent is such a valuable thing. Often, due to lack of opportunity, a good story is missed, a good storyteller overlooked. For the Litchfield Writer's Group, this, fortunately hasn't been the case. They tell it well.
-- Cindy Swenson, Proprietress, Lulu Beans Coffee House, Willmar

Another outstanding project by members of the Litchfield Area Writer's Group. That this small group has been together so long and continue to tell stories that make us laugh, cry, and wait anxiously for the next book in the annual series is simply incredible.
-- Brent Schacherer, Editor, Litchfield Independent Review

Interesting, insightful, real life stories.
-- Steve Linder, President of Lakeland Broadcasting Company, Willmar

A View From The Verandah

A View From the Verandah

Writing by Members of the Litchfield Area Writers Group

Edited by Julianne Johnson

A View From The Verandah

ISBN: 0-9710796-9-2
LCCN:

Published by Filbert Publishing, Box 326, Kandiyohi, Mn, 56251, USA and Cricket Meadow Press, Grove City, Mn, 56243. No part of this publication may be reproduced, stored in a retrieval system, or transmitted in any form or by any means, electronic, mechanical, recording or otherwise, without the prior written permission of the authors. The authors have individual copyrights on each story.

Manufactured in the United States of America.

Cover Photo: Sharon Oakes
Blackberry Farm
Walland, TN

A View From the Verandah

Writing by Members of the Litchfield Area Writers Group

Edited by Julianne Johnson

A View From The Verandah

Dedication

This book is dedicated to Patrik Mattsson, a longtime member and friend of our group. Patrik is suffering from a debilitating illness that prevents him from attending our meetings. But we feel his presence with us. Though he can't be among us, we consider him to be a member still. His courage and patience have been an inspiration to us all.

Table of Contents

Elizabeth Bergstrom

Tim Bergstrom

Mildred Hummel

Julianne J. Johnson

9

A View From The Verandah

A View From The Verandah

A View From the Verandah

Introduction

In this busy, hustle-bustle age when people barely have time to breathe, it seems we need each other more than ever before and that time is our most prized commodity. It seems that pulling up a chair on the back porch, sipping a drink and sharing a story, is just what the doctor ordered.

Our views, shared here in this book, are from our individual verandahs, each seeing or experiencing things differently yet, in many ways, coming to the same conclusions, realizing the same end result.

We hope you enjoy our musings where we recall our favored thoughts, our fondest memories, our worst nightmares. They're all a part of who we are, what we've become. Our view may not be your view but come, "set a spell," we want to share it all with you.

Julianne Johnson

Elizabeth M. Bergstrom

Bette's first glimpse of life was in 1921 at an old Victorian house in Grove City. Bette always loved stories and started to write when in grade school. At age nine, she wrote a book called "The Old Scratch House." She sent installments of this story to her sister Virginia, who was confined to Eitel Hospital in Minneapolis for three months. She received Bette's complete story before she was due to come home. Bette attended all twelve grades of school in Grove City and then went on to St. Cloud Teachers College for two years. World War II interrupted plans to be a teacher, so she filled a vacancy as a bookkeeper at the local bank where her father and brother both worked. After flipping a coin, Bette and three Grove City friends headed east (instead of west) to work in government jobs. Two years in Washington, D.C. during the feverish time of the war provided unique experiences. Later, Bette returned to Minnesota and married a farmer, Oliver Bergstrom, who had just been discharged from the navy. They were married 43 years, lived on three different farms in Meeker County and raised four children. She spends her time reading, writing, and enjoying her 6 grandchildren and her cottage at the lake.

The Bad Penny Turns Up

When I had bid goodnight to the sailor I had dated that sultry July night in Washington, D.C., I opened our apartment door and was greeted with a strange sight. There was Marcella, my roommate, with a satisfied grin on her face as she pointed to the soldier she had gone out with on a blind date that evening. He was securely tied to a sturdy dining room chair with many feet of stout rope. His arms were tied behind him and his feet were tied together. He was red-faced and sweating profusely in a struggle to free himself.

"Let me go, you witch," he bellowed.

"Marcie, what is going on?" I asked. "Why this treatment?" "This is the only way I could handle him. It's like having a date with an octopus!"

Marcella was the athletic type, built like an Amazon. She had worked on her family's farm. It was a large family of mostly girls. She was proud of her strength, and she lifted the man and chair together to prove it.

It was extremely funny, so I laughed!

He rocked the chair, making no headway.

"You, woman witch," he addressed me. "Get a scissors and help me. This is not funny! If my platoon leader hears that I am injured, you're in trouble!" he groaned.

He looked weak and was embarrassed to be controlled by a woman.

This ill-fated evening definitely was the result of a BLIND date, I thought as I looked him over. He looked like a cartoon in the funny paper!

He had two sizes of ears, dark brown eyes as hard and expressionless as two marbles, one eye cocked with no expression except disgust. His bumpy nose was pushed to one side like a prize fighter's. He had unhealthy-looking gray-white skin with blue joints stretched tight. He had bunches of dusty-looking tight blonde curls. I won't forget that look ever!

"Marcie, where did you get all this nice rope?" I murmured with a puzzled look.

"Oh, I keep this on hand for just such purposes as this!"

"Oh," was all I could answer, remembering how I learned to tie knots in Girl Scouts. I admitted it could be a good thing to know.

"Marcie, you'd better untie him and let him go. He might pass out from the heat or even die. Then you'd be in trouble with the U.S.Government."

She did untie some of the knots and even cut some of the worst ones.

As soon as he was free, he shot out of the apartment like a pea out of a pea shooter.

"Well, we won't see him again!" exclaimed Marcie with a low chuckle.

Two years later, I had moved back to Minnesota and was employed as a receptionist at the Bureau of Veterans' Affairs on the campus of the University of Minnesota. This job involved referring veterans to a counselor and helping them get their books and other supplies under the GI Bill. I met many former service men in this capacity, and I enjoyed my work.

One day I looked at the two long lines of vets. Evelyn Nesvold and I each were in charge of one line.

Then the unexpected happened!

My eyes caught sight of the face of "Bob Bender", the bad penny from Washington, D.C. I hoped he didn't recognize me.

With pounding heart, I said, "Evie, will you switch places with me? I must avoid this one man."

She looked puzzled but said, "O.K."

As he came closer, I didn't even glance at him with his hungry, troubled look. I felt sorry for him when I thought of it, but I didn't get carried away by pity.

I didn't look at the other line until I realized he had been sent to a counselor. But now he was in line with my desk. Soon it was lunch time, and I could breathe easier. So I took my bag lunch and headed down the path to the cliff above the Mississippi River. It was a beautiful fall day, and I looked forward to the scenic walk. The path I took was somewhat precarious, with crumbling clay walls and rocky footing. I felt good about getting out of sight. Just as I found a niche in the clay bank to sit on, that face showed up above the edge of the bluff, and he yelled, "Hi! Remember me?"

Oh, no, I thought as I shrank back into the clay niche, must I deal with that creep?

He kept hanging over and said, "I know you. Your name is Bette." Then he disappeared from sight. I was sure he was groping for the path and would soon be down to my level.

My heart was pounding and I felt desperate.

A few minutes later some students came along the shore walking. Three boys and two girls. I didn't know them but I boldly addressed them. This was my chance for a getaway so I approached them.

"You've got to help me! Someone is following me, an undesirable character, and I must give him the slip. I work at Shevlin Hall."

"Sure. You can come with us. We've got an old jalopy parked up at the top. We'll give you a ride to Shevlin Hall.."

I was so grateful for their help! We climbed the path to the top together like we were old friends, and this scared Bob away for the time being. As we met him, he turned away.

He popped in two more times at the Vet's Bureau, but I eluded him each time. I haven't seen him since, but I've never forgotten the strange face or the dilemma he caused. It comes back to me sometimes in a dream.

Junior

I caught a whiff of flower-scented summer breezes reminding me of lovely days and nights spent at Green Lake.

It was June in Washington, D.C., and the city was enduring extremely high heat and humidity.

I missed the summer water activities, so much a part of my growing-up years. Here there was only the smell of water if you got close enough to the Tidal Basin or the Potomac River.

Early in the summer a neighbor of ours introduced me to a handsome marine sergeant. He invited me to go on a moonlight cruise on a river boat. He was respectful to me and fun to be with. So I thought, "This will be a good summer."

After two months, I found out he had a wife in Florida! I made an abrupt end to that affair. I can't believe seemingly nice men can't be trusted!

The next day at work I complained to my good friend Florence about my dilemma.

"I'm sick of this! Who can I trust?"

"Well," she answered, "I know one for sure that you could trust. He is my nephew, Inez's boy. I can guarantee you can trust him. His name is Junior."

"What's his real name?" I asked.

"Junior is his name. That's all."

I was a little dubious about anyone with this name who is grown up.

"I'll call him and tell him about you," Florence offered.

"O. K.," I agreed. "I'll go for it if he is interested."

"I can tell you one thing. He's decent. He's a gentleman," she repeated.

Florence called him and set up a date for the coming Friday evening.

When Friday evening came, I dressed up in a white sailor dress with navy blue accessories, all set for an evening on the water.

When Junior came to the door with a bold knock, I opened and thought, "He is so nervous he can't stand still."

He kept running his fingers through his tight curly hair.

"You ready? Let's go." He snapped his gum.

"Oh, no," I thought. "He chews bubble gum and keeps snapping it. How appropriate for someone named Junior. He'll blow a big bubble and it will cover his whole face. Grow up, Junior!"

Well, I mustn't go by first impressions.

"Come on! Let's go," he repeated abruptly.

"Where are we going?" I asked.

"To the movies," he answered as he snapped his fingers.

What else does he snap? I wondered.

"I really wanted to go for a canoe ride on the Potomac."

"Oh, do you?" he answered. "I don't know anything about canoeing."

"Well, it's still and it's moonlight, "I answered enthusiastically. "It would be perfect. I'll help you."

I thought to myself as he hesitated, "Maybe he thinks it's too expensive. Should I offer to pay half? Would he be insulted?"

"I suppose we can try it," he said.

"I just love the sound and smell of water," I commented. "I grew up living by a lake."

As we bounced along in the bus, I asked, "What do you like to do?"

"Nothing much," was the reply.

That was dull, I thought. "Do you like to read?"

"Oh, no," was a definite answer.

"Do you go biking? Or hiking?"

"No!"

"Marbles?" I said kiddingly, but he didn't think it was funny.

Then I asked curiously, "Do you swim?"

"No," he admitted reluctantly.

No wonder he didn't like my choice of entertainment for the evening.

We arrived at the canoe rental place and stepped into a red canoe as Junior handed some money to the attendant. He was extremely nervous about being on water in this tippy craft. I showed him what I knew about paddling. We drifted with the current. When we were out in the middle of the river, Junior suddenly lunged at me in an awkward embrace! I was shocked at his nerve and lack of manners. Florence's words echoed in my head, "He's a gentleman."

Then standing up uneasily, Junior grabbed for me again. I gave him a shove, and the canoe was wavering before it leveled again in the ripples of the river.

"Be careful, Buddy," I threatened. "I can rock this canoe and easily upset it."

He had no finesse or even decent courtesy. I held the dripping paddle upright, dripping water on Junior's curly hair.

"If we tip over, I can swim to shore, but what would you do?"

He stared at me in disbelief.

"Aunt Florence said you were a nice person."

"I can be when I'm treated right," I countered, holding my paddle upright threateningly, dripping more water onto Junior. He hated water like a cat!

I paddled the canoe back to shore with no more conversation. We rode the bus back to my apartment in silence. At least, he had quit snapping his fingers and his gum.

Junior grabbed me rudely again at the door. I gave him a shove.

"Thanks," I murmured. "Find your type somewhere else. I'm not it!"

At work on Monday, I explained the whole incident to Florence, who looked puzzled.

"He certainly had me fooled!" she exclaimed.

Treasures From The Shore

At random times during the year, I pick up Anne Lindbergh's "Gift from the Sea" and enjoy her thoughts and moods.

I agree that the beach is not a place for mental discipline, but it is an ideal spot to let thoughts wander sometimes into the past, often dwelling on the present or the future. It's a setting where the mind can be a blank page, and the beach can inspire some ideas.

Often my thoughts take me into the past where I spent happy childhood hours with seemingly endless summer days. I had the freedom to run the smooth, sandy shoreline enjoying a marathon of splattering foam from the restless waves that covered me and anything in my path. I could flit like a butterfly, pausing to enjoy treasures washed up by the waves.

Sometimes I would push the old wooden rowboat out into the lake, jump in and just exult in drifting with no port in mind. Such freedom brought feelings of joy which I have not experienced since.

Days of adult responsibility crowded into my life. Now when I am older and have shared in farm work and raised a family, I realize life could be so simple and satisfying with just attaining the basics of food, clothing, and shelter. Of course, that wouldn't be enough because we need social stimulation and books to read. I would feel deprived if I didn't have a book within reach at all times.

Morning at the beach is inspiring and is my favorite time wherever I am. Early hours give a new start and fresh outlook.

When I search the sands and find an agate, I feel triumphant. I favor the reddish ones with faint white stripes. They should be transparent so light shines through.

These are more scarce now than when I was a child. Maybe the harsh winter with tons of ice heaving up on the shore has changed the contents of the beach sand.

Even now there are jet black stones to be found, and the white limestone ones can be used to write messages. We left messages for the future, but of course those were obliterated over winter every year.

The new cobblestone fireplace at our lake cottage contains four unique rocks picked by my mother for the mantel of their brick fireplace built in 1920. We rescued these to be included in the new one, and now her great-grandchildren can point to them with pride.

Another shore activity is to search for interesting pieces of driftwood. The shape and smoothness tell a story more intriguing than sculptures made by man.

At the end of a morning of musings, I clutch a bag of stones, shells, and driftwood to bring up to the cabin. I've only chosen the very special ones to keep. This gives me an example of how to simplify other collections and keepsakes so clutter cannot alter the enjoyment of a few rare things.

Thanks, Anne Lindbergh, for timeless inspiration!

The Rest Of The Story

There is a certain stretch of country road several miles north of here that I'll always remember. I would like to think of it as a place of scenic beauty, but it brings an unpleasant memory of a close call; an unexpected event that could have caused injury or even death.

My mother-in-law, Mabel Bergstrom Jacobson, had asked me if I could give her a ride to a well-known faith healer, Mrs. Oliver, who lived in a humble house on the far west street in Hawick, Minnesota. Mabel had been there before for treatment of some kidney ailment.

It was a beautiful day in May of 1951. My day was free and our car was available. I enjoyed driving the country roads in the springtime. We had reached a series of curves in the road by the Nordland Church, when an old beat-up blue car came rolling in front of us too fast. Trying to get straightened out, the car landed in the left-hand ditch, came back across the road to the right hand ditch, and ended up in the left ditch upside down. I managed to avoid him by some miracle.

I stopped the car holding my breath and looked at Mabel who was speechless, too. Finally she said, "We'll have to see if he's hurt."

There were no seat belts in those days. The driver staggered out in a daze and fell in the long grass of the ditch. Mabel recognized him as one of her neighbors who was often drunk, even early in the day.

"Why, it's Gjertson Gunderson!" she said.

"Are you sure that's his name?" I asked, thinking to myself, "who would name a baby Gjertson? He would have a strike against him even at birth".

Mabel stayed with him in the grassy ditch while I drove to a nearby farm place to get help. The farmer wasn't surprised when he saw him, bleeding from a head wound, and said, "I'll take him to the doctor as he has some cuts and bruises."

The farmer commented, "He's done this before." I could have guessed that by the condition of his car.

"He's so relaxed, he doesn't get hurt much," the farmer added.

"Someone should keep him at home. He's a menace on the road," I commented.

"He has no one at home," I was told.

I thought to myself, "So-is the driving public supposed to take chances with him on the road? It's like playing Russian Roulette."

After he was taken care of, Mabel and I continued on to Hawick.

"Maybe we aren't meant to go to the healer," I suggested with a smile. But we kept going and found the yard full of cars. There were no appointments. You just waited your turn.

When Mabel was done with her session, she had some white handkerchiefs with her. "These have been blessed," she explained.

"Then what do you do with them?"

"Put them wherever you have painful aches. Would you like to try a treatment for your eczema on your eyelids and neck?"

I thought it over and decided, "O.K. I'll try it as long as we're here and still alive."

I remember Mrs. Oliver's gentle touch as she touched my eyes. With her eyes closed, she concentrated on the problem areas.

A few days passed and I hadn't given it much thought, but the eczema mysteriously had gone away, and it has never come back. I couldn't say it didn't work because I had the proof.

I go by this ditch quite often when going to Green Lake or Lost Valley.

I start to comment "this is where"-but don't need to finish because all the family knows the rest of the story.

Tim Bergstrom

Tim Bergstrom joined the staff at KLFD AM 1410 radio in Litchfield in 1995 and is the station's news director. He was elected president of the Minnesota Associated Press broadcasters board of directors this past year. He's a member of First Baptist Church in Grove City, The Litchfield Area Tourism Association, and The Peanut Butter and Milk Festival Committee. Besides writing, Tim enjoys reading, biking, skiing, gardening, cooking, going to plays and movies, and traveling. His 2003 travels included a month in Australia.

The Benzene Cafe

My playhouse as a child was in a most unusual location - underneath the gas barrel used by my father to fuel his tractors and trucks on our farm. The large silver barrel was perched atop a wooden frame and made a perfect home for my pretend cafe. Mom gave me her discarded pots, pans and silverware which I hung on the boards supporting the gas barrel.

The structure was located just a few yards east of the kitchen window where Mom spent hours washing dishes, peeling potatoes, canning fruits and vegetables, and keeping an eye on me. She was often a good sport and took time away from her chores to patronize my cafe.

Mud pies were the specialty at my restaurant which was located right next to a massive, hollow box elder tree. I lined my pie tins with box elder leaves from the tree for the crust and then filled it in with a runny mixture of mud and other debris.

When I got tired of cooking and waiting on my customer, I spent time in a huge tractor tire next to the gas barrel/restaurant which Dad had filled with gravel for a makeshift sandbox. Our barn cats enjoyed the sandbox too. I unearthed several of their droppings over the years which made perfect frankfurters for my menu.

Occasionally, I got to serve as a filling station attendant as Dad would drive up with his model A John Deere or our old Dodge truck and need a fill-up. My filling station/restaurant also had a restroom in the back.

The back of the box elder tree was a perfect place for a boy to take a leak - with the hollow portion serving as a urinal. One day, Ken Allen and Peggy Erickson - friends of my brother and sister, drove up while I was in midstream. I was pretty embarrassed and didn't use my open-air restroom much after that.

My oldest brother, Phil, backed into my cafe one day - causing the gas barrel to fall into the roof of our brown Rambler. I was sent, along with my siblings, Juli and Dan, to bed early that night so Dad could have a talk with Phil.

Due to the end of my childhood, the death of the tree and the relocation of the gas barrel to the side of our garage, my restaurant business kind of died off. I re-opened in a new location with a new name, Reggie's Restaurant, but it just wasn't the same.

I don't know if the exposure to the gasoline during my childhood had any ill effects on my health. We didn't think much about those things back then. The memories of the fun I had creatively playing in the Benzene Cafe will stay with me for as long as I live.

Christmas Family Tree

As I dismantled the Christmas tree today, I analyzed each ornament as it was packed away for another year. Each one has a story behind it and most of them have connections to members of my family and special friends.

One of the oldest ornaments is a star that perched at the top of each Christmas tree during my childhood. It looks kind of like a small version of those glass-mirrored balls that were common at disco dances in the 1970s. It has pink-colored points and a large silver point at the top. I've seen the same one in antique stores.

Another old ornament is a glass Santa Claus that used to be on the tree in the house of my Uncle George and Aunt Virginia. My grandparents probably had it on their tree earlier in the 1900s. I'm now living in the same house, so the ornament has returned home. The Santa has a silver face, red suit with frosted white trim, and he's holding a little green Christmas tree. My sister, Juli, gave me a similar glass ornament about ten years ago of Santa's head. He has a silver face, red cap, blue eyes and a white, frosted beard.

My aunt Virginia picked up several ornaments at the Emmaus Gift Shop in Litchfield during the two years that she was a resident of Bethany home in the late 1970s. I have several of those ornaments on my tree. My favorite is a pair of white felt ice skates. The blades on the skates are actually large silver paper clips.

Ornaments made by my nieces and nephew have hung on my tree over the years. One of them is a wreath made with scraps of fabric. Several of my ornaments have been made by friends. My KLFD coworker, Peg Smith, made three ornaments that are very special to me. They are styrofoam balls with fabric sewed on to them. Each has a small rose stuck in near the top and one has a small string of pearls for a hanging loop. My friend, Mary Alice Holm, made me a cloth ornament this year of a snowman with a carrot nose. My friend, LaNae Osmond, gave me an ornament one year that looks like a birdhouse quilt. Another year she gave me three little penguin figurines that have hung on my tree ever since.

My cousin's daughter, Molly Bergstrom, gave me a small Hallmark penguin about 20 years ago. It is carefully packed back in its little keepsake box each year and is stored in my desk. My cousin, Melissa, made four cloth ornaments for our family one year with cross-stitching. One says "Peace," another says "Joy," one has a small wreath, and the other has Santa.

My cousin, Nancy, who operates a business in Alaska called Wooly Paws, made two little stockings that hang on my tree. My Uncle Al and Aunt Gerri in Alaska sent us an ornament one year that was carved out of olive wood in Bethlehem. It has a figure kneeling and praying next to a cross. I bought an ornament while visiting my cousin, Allen, one year in Los Angeles. We ate lunch at Jack in the Box, and I purchased an ornament with Jack riding on a reindeer.

My cousins' grandmother, Mabel Wilson of Hawick, crocheted a green and red stocking that always hangs on our Christmas tree. One of her daughters, Marguerite Hufford, made several ornaments out of old jewelry and gave them to my mother. They resemble a bell, a star and an icicle. One of the newest ornaments on my tree is from Hufford's church, United Methodist of Hawick. They had a live nativity in 2002 and handed out paper ornaments with a stamp of the baby Jesus and a small spike glued to the front, and a poem on the back explaining the significance of Christ's birth, death and resurrection. Another prized home-made ornament was made by a longtime member of my church Martha Peterson. It's a square, cloth ornament with a Christmas tree sewn in the middle.

While I taught Sunday School at First Baptist Church in Grove City, one of my students, Stacey Laidlaw, gave me a little brown bear ornament. The red-vested critter has hung on my tree ever since. We've made several ornaments at my church over the years during Advent services. One of them is an angel made out of various kinds of pasta, with paper wings - spray-painted white, and holding a golden harp. Another one is a cradle made of popsicle sticks and a little baby Jesus inside. Another one has a picture of the baby Jesus glued inside a little box, with yarn glued to the bottom to look like straw, a little paper sheep glued on top of the yarn, and a fence across the opening of the box made of toothpicks. It has a 3-dimensional look. One of the missionaries supported by my church, Sara Hewitt, sent a red and white ribbon made of thread one year from Bulgaria. I forget what it symbolized, but it reminds me to pray for her whenever I see it.

I bought a small Pinocchio ornament while shopping in the quaint little village of Rothenburg, Germany. There are several Land 'O' Lakes ornaments on my tree from the era when my brother, Phil, worked for that company. One of the most unique ornaments in that collection is a wooden oval ornament from 1990 with a butter churn carved in the middle. I have one ornament leftover from the time my friend, Trish Ramme, sold all of her worldly possessions and moved from Litchfield, Minnesota to Anchorage, Alaska. It's just a ball made of gold elastic chords with a tassel on the bottom. It was in a box of items to be discarded. I've kept it to remember Trish.

Several of my ornaments were acquired when Suzie's went out of business in downtown Litchfield, and when Teske's expanded its store in the Litchfield Shopping Center and became a Hallmark dealer. One of those stores had wooden garlands resembling a string of peppermint candies, and garlands of glass ornaments that resemble the old-fashioned Christmas lights. Those garlands are wrapped around my tree each year.

These are just a few of the ornaments that hang on my tree each year. Many special ornaments have broken over the years, and some have been discarded. Just about anything that can be hooked has a chance of being placed on my Christmas tree.

Coincidence In A Small World

I stumbled upon the scene of an accident today (11/3/1993) in Austin, Minnesota which in itself could be the groundwork for a great story, but the man I met and our connections to Litchfield are what really moved me to write about this incident.

Three times a week, I religiously walk one mile each way to the YMCA and work-out on weight machines. My usual route takes me east on 10th Avenue and then south on 1st Drive Northwest.

I had just started my walk and was approaching the intersection of 10th Avenue and 11th Street and saw a confusing scene. There was a car (an Olds Cutlass Ciera) "parked" in front of a tree, a young Vietnamese woman talking frantically and an older gentleman trying to calm her. As I got closer, I saw the young woman rush to a nearby house, trying to get into the front door. I saw an older Vietnamese woman slumped in the driver's seat, and realized there had been an accident, so I ran across the street to try to help. The young woman shouted to the older man, "There's no one home! I can't call for help!" "I'll run to another house," replied the man.

The young woman then noticed me as she held a white rag to the older woman's head and pulled her out of the seat. "She has a hole in her head!" the young woman shouted to me.

I could see the cracked windshield of the car, a bloody rag, and blood spattered all over the woman's white jacket. As queasy as I felt, I said to the young woman, "Just let her sit back in the seat. I'll try to get help from another house." I ran across the street, and then another man yelled to the older man and me, "I called 9-1-1 already!" We assured the young woman that an ambulance was on its way.

The grill of the car was smashed-in at least a foot with the trunk of a large cedar tree in the center of the car's path. About ten feet away stood a lucky, unscathed house with no one at home. A large pool of lime green anti-freeze formed on the sidewalk. Neither, the older man nor I witnessed the accident, but discussed several theories of its cause prior to the arrival of the police.

"I bet she tromped on the gas pedal instead of the brakes when she got to the stop sign, and then panicked," the older man said.

"Maybe the cruise control button was activated and she couldn't figure out how to turn it off," I added.

"Perhaps the gas pedal stuck," replied the man.

With our theories exhausted, the police and ambulance arrived. They quickly got everything under control, and since the man and I had not witnessed the accident, we were free to leave the scene.

"I was on my way to my office downtown," said the man.

"I was on my way to the Y," I replied.

"Well, hop in my car. I'll give you a ride," he said.

Once he started driving down the street, he introduced himself, "I'm John Sperry."

"My name is Tim Bergstrom," I replied and added, "Nice to meet you, John." "Do you go to school, Tim?" he asked.

"Yes, I'm attending Riverland Technical College," I said, then added, "Are you a native of Austin, John?"

"I'm originally from Minneapolis, but have lived here in Austin for 40 years. I'm a dental surgeon, and since I'm 76, I'm basically retired," he said.

When he introduced himself, I thought he said his name was John Sparboe so I asked, "Do you have any connection to Sparboe Farms in Litchfield?"

"Yes," he replied, "My son, Steve Sperry, is an attorney and represents Sparboe Farms!"

It was then that I realized how amazing this coincidence was. I would have never asked him the Sparboe question if I'd heard his name correctly. Sperry is not an unusual name, but I've not heard of the name Sparboe except for the egg company in Litchfield. And I wasn't aware that Steve Sperry represented Sparboe Farms.

As John dropped me off at the YMCA, I had nearly forgotten about the accident scene where we met. "I hope if we meet again, John, it's under more pleasant circumstances," I said.

And that was my coincidence in a small world. By the way, I planned to fry a hamburger for supper, but after seeing that accident scene, I decided to make macaroni and cheese instead.

Norma

Central Minnesota lost a broadcasting legend on March 31, 2003. Norma Berke had reported the Litchfield Area

News on KDUZ radio for over 40 years, retiring in 1996. I had the privilege of sitting with Norma at the media table at a few Litchfield City Council meetings before her career ended. She worked on a few special projects for my employer, KLFD, in the late 1990s - including interviews with the Alabama guests during the annual Peanut Butter and Milk Festival, and sharing recipes with our listeners before the Christmas holiday season.

One of the tricks of the broadcasting trade is to keep obituaries on file of celebrities - before they die - so that when they pass away, you have the information available instantly. This isn't a big concern in a small community like Litchfield, but I put together a tribute to Norma Berke in the event that she would die. In my mind, she was our local celebrity, and I wanted to make sure she was remembered. It became standard procedure any time I would go on vacation, to remind the rest of the staff, that if anything happened to Norma, they were to use the story I had on file in my desk. It was sad when I finally retrieved the story on April 1st of 2003.

I once told Norma how my father would stop any work he was doing on the farm at 10 o'clock every weekday morning so he could listen to her news. I wasn't so interested in the news as a youngster, but was grateful to Norma for the break she gave me from the farm work.

Norma would have the latest news from the Sheriff's and Police Departments, the funeral notices, hospital admissions, discharges and births and much more. She often shared recipes and published several cookbooks over the years containing those recipes. She broadcast the news right from her home and her reports were often interrupted by her dog barking, the UPS man ringing the doorbell or some other occurrence which added to the charm of her reports.

A few months after I took over the news department at KLFD, and when Norma left KDUZ in 1996, someone found out who I was and commented sarcastically, "So you're the one who replaced Norma Berke." That wasn't quite true as we worked for different radio stations, but in a way, I was flattered that someone would compare our mission of keeping people informed. More recently someone described me as the new Norma Berke. Again, I was flattered. Norma was a class-act. If someone writes my obituary before I die, then perhaps I'll be in the same class as Norma.

Remembering Skip

He was a fixture in the city of Spicer. He was as much a part of the local coffee shop as the coffee maker itself. This resident was Hervey Martin, known affectionately as "Skip."

Skip was a small man, probably about 5 feet tall and maybe a shade over 100 pounds. He wore big glasses, or maybe they just looked big on his small face. He always wore a visor cap so I couldn't tell you whether or not he was bald, but the hair on the back of his head was dark as was his complexion. He usually wore flannel shirts, a windbreaker and blue jeans. He crossed his feet and bent his legs toward the back of his chair, giving him the appearance of a small boy.

I didn't know Skip personally, only as an observer. If he walked down the sidewalk and I happened to be working nearby, he'd pause and may, "Hi! How's it going?" I tried to make it a point to say "hello" to him whenever I'd enter the coffee shop. He'd usually sit alone at a small table near the door.

In October of 1991, Skip was uncharacteristically absent from the coffee shop.

He passed away at Rice Hospital on October 30, the result of a heart attack at age 64.

He died right before the big Halloween blizzard. He was survived by two sisters and I thought of stopping by the funeral home to show them my support, but due to the storm, was snowed in near Grove City. All I could think about was the small showing of mourners there would be to remember Skip because of the weather.

Skip's grave is in the northwest part of the old cemetery in Spicer next to the Iverson headstone, under an ash tree. When it was sodded this past spring, it was the most fertile looking area in the whole cemetery. The combination of morning sun, afternoon shade and ample rains made the grass very lush.

As I was mowing the cemetery one day in mid-August, it dawned on me that Skip had no grave marker yet; not even a flower to mark his grave. I felt bad about this so I went to the utility shed where we put unclaimed flowers in the fall. I found a clump of red silk roses and stuck them on Skip's plot. It was a small gesture, but I felt that the long time Spicer "landmark" should be remembered.

I'll always remember you Skip, if not with a secondhand bouquet, then at least in my heart.

Mildred Hummel

Many of Mildred's stories center around the people and events in Litchfield and Meeker County. She is in a good position to write these memories because she grew up in the Kingston area and, after marrying Al Hummel and working with him in the Litchfield Gamble Store many years, was well aware of happenings in the community. Mildred realizes the importance of recording the history of the community. She has enjoyed being a member of the Litchfield Area Writers Group for the past ten years and has appreciated the part the G.A.R. Hall and Museum has played in promoting the books the group has published by holding public readings for each new book.

My Birthday Dress

My birthday was coming up - and my mother was willing to make me a new dress - I knew that!

So, we went to Iver Peterson's store in Kingston where there were bolts of cloth available. Satin-type cloth that was blue in color.

I had told her that I really wanted a dress with a plain top and a skirt filled with ruffles all around the skirt. She accepted that challenge and did it.

My mother didn't have a ruffler on her machine at that time - but she was an experienced dress maker. She cut strips of material on the bias (she said) and hemmed one side of the ruffle. Then she stitched the other side and pulled the threads through the top and somehow sewed these ruffles on the skirt!

I was delighted and would parade around showing it off.
My brother, Irving, didn't appreciate that much. He said,
"This is a dumb idea!"

Up the Hill to Set The Bread

My mother and father, Emily Loftness and John Justeson,
became engaged on July 4, 1912.

They were married on September 29 on my grandfather
Enok Loftness' 75th birthday, in his home in Gibbon,
Minnesota the same year.

A few days after the wedding, they returned together by train to
the North Kingston area where my father still lived with his parents,
Iver and Christine Justeson and another brother, Peter.

My grandfather, Iver, was getting older so John and Peter
did most of the work.

My grandmother, Christine, did most of the housework and
was definitely in charge of the house!

My dad had purchased 120 acres and the adjoining farm
home after he became engaged to my mother.

After the wedding festivities were celebrated in Gibbon,
they returned by train to the Iver Justeson farm together, but
the farm buildings on the farm my father had purchased were
badly in need of repair - so my father brought his bride home to
his parental home because the weather was becoming colder -
and there was much fall work to accomplish.

Now there were two capable women in one kitchen - but it was
my grandmother's kitchen and she was definitely in charge! This
went on for some time and grandmother daily gave orders to my
mother.

This, of course, did not fare too well with Emily, my mother.

Emily was becoming more and more agitated, but she did
not want to start an argument with her mother-in-law, Christine

Justeson. The day came, however, when my mother Emily had heard enough. Emily had been a professional fashion designer and dressmaker in a ladies ready-to-wear shop near the capitol in St. Paul before her marriage to my father.

She had been secretly preparing her kitchen in the vacant house on the hill for moving, but it was growing colder and my father kept postponing the move!

Then, one day grandmother ordered Emily, "Run down to the old house and bring me a pail."

That's the day my mother didn't want to start arguing with my grandmother. She went into the pantry instead, put some yeast in her pocket, walked up to the house on the hill and set the bread.

When my father came into the house, he inquired, "Har ar Emilie?" ("Where is Emily?") Grandmother replied in Swedish, because she never learned to speak English, "Har yek uppa bechen."("She walked up the hill!")

My father ran up the hill and found my mother cleaning the kitchen. She wasted no time, she simply said, "I have moved!"

My grandfather, Iver Justeson, had realized that two women in one kitchen wasn't working out too well, so he had gone to their wall telephone and called the other relatives who lived nearby and said, "Emily has moved."

Grandpa's word was like the law in our family. It had to be obeyed so everyone he called responded by coming at once.

They brought their horses and wagons - hammers, nails and everything needed to make improvements as directed by my grandfather and Uncle August Nystrom. Both of these men were experienced carpenters. They gave the orders - and my grandfather had plenty of lumber so improvements were made on all the building within a few days.

Then came the day when half of the cows, horses, pigs and chickens and machinery were carted up the hill one way or another. My father and his brother Peter split their holdings peacefully.

My mother kept the coffee pot on the kitchen range hot and had managed to bake a lot of cinnamon rolls which she served to keep the workers well fed.

This is how this young, newly-married couple moved up the hill.

All because my mother put some yeast in her pocket, walked up the hill and set the bread!

We Were In Church

We were in church when Pearl Harbor was attacked.

Al and I were attending a service at the Ostmark Lutheran Church for an evening of worship. Hymns had been sung and the pastor was already in the pulpit preaching.

Suddenly an usher came quietly up the aisle and whispered something to the pastor. The pastor responded, "I have been informed that the Japanese have just bombed Pearl Harbor (the chief U.S. Naval Base in Hawaii). Many ships have been sunk and many local residents, as well as servicemen, have been killed by this action."

Then Al whispered to me, "I will have to go."

The pastor was visibly sad and responded by saying, "Let us all pray!" After that, we quietly left the church and could not imagine what the consequences would be for our family.

It was then that our lives began to change. Al anticipated it all before I realized what it would mean to us as a family.

At his suggestion, I returned to St. Cloud Teacher's College to renew my certification as a teacher. I drove back and forth from Litchfield to St. Cloud and attended classes for six weeks.

I usually left our daughter Elaine off at my parents farm, eight miles from Kimball. Her grandparents were delighted to have her.

Then, I would stop at the farm and pick her up and drive back to town. Very often my mother would send along a hotdish for supper for us.

I completed the necessary courses in six weeks. Teachers are required to keep up their certification. After that I applied and was hired to teach at District 8, about eight miles south of Litchfield.

Al did everything that he decided was necessary. He put our house up for sale and rented an apartment near main street for us. He moved the furniture we needed to take for a small apartment and found a lady who would come to the apartment at 7 o'clock, as I had to leave then for work in the school.

I was sad that I had to miss Elaine's first day at school, but Elaine didn't mind. She liked Mrs. Jenson and was comfortable with her husband, too. I couldn't get home until 5 o'clock, so they took care of her when she came home from school, too. She thought about them like grandparents - and they felt that way, too. I taught in District 8 one year.

Al came back home for a three week leave after he completed Basic Training. He said it had been a tough course - up at 5 and going through all sorts of exercises, marching for miles and learning to swim.

He grew up in North Dakota and there were no lakes nearby. Anyhow, he managed to pass that test.

As a side effect of the water training, he had developed a hearing loss. He came home anyway, and had refused seeing the Navy doctor, as he didn't trust him. So, when he came home, he immediately went to see a doctor he trusted, Dr. Harold Wilmot, who treated him at once by removing some water in his inner ear. We were very grateful.

I recall a funny incident during his leave. I had invited Ruth and Len Hobert over for dinner. As it happened, Leonard was being treated for an ear infection too, and when they conversed they talked so loud that Ruth and I adjourned to the living room away from the kitchen. Anyway, they both received their normal hearing again.

When Al returned to Navy headquarters, he was assigned to a ship, the U.S.S. Laport, that carried troops into battle. His duty aboard the ship was "The Store Keeper." It was a small room on the second deck and featured some magazines, books, candy bars, cigarettes, stationery, pens. etc. He recalled that everything had to be done at certain hours. The store had to be opened at 7 a.m. and closed at 5 sharp in the afternoon.

One morning a General officer came by at 6:45 a.m. and ordered, "Sailor, open the store for me!" Al saluted and replied, "Sir, I can not open the store until 7 o'clock sharp."

The General called an assistant and said, "Take this sailor to the brig!" So he spent the night on a cot in the jail. In the morning the General appeared and said, "Release the sailor. I was testing him to see how he would respond!"

Al was really disgusted because if he had opened the door of the ship's store for the General, he would have been in worse trouble!

Al learned that the U.S.S. LaPorte would be commissioned in Seattle and return to Seattle after leaving the troops off near Okinawa, so after a year he wanted us to come stay in Seattle because I had an uncle and Aunt Minnie living there. So, I didn't sign a contract to teach, but the school board was understanding so Elaine and I stayed with my uncle and aunt.

We all attended the commissioning of the ship. I remember the sailors had been lined up for an hour before the General arrived, and as he came aboard they all had to salute him at once! Quite a scene - no cameras were allowed.

Whenever the ship returned, Al was able to hitch-hike to Aunt Minnie's to be with us. Aunt Minnie was a wonderful cook and she made an early breakfast especially for him. She cooked oatmeal, fried eggs and made pancakes, as well as fresh fruit! One day when Al had leave for a day, they let us use their car so Al and I could drive around together. Elaine stayed with them.

I think we were in Seattle with them for a month or two. Then the ship's captain decided to put up troops in Astoria, Oregon. Aunt Minnie called the Lutheran Church there and found a place for Elaine and me in an apartment building where there was one apartment downstairs and one upstairs. The downstairs one was occupied by Ruby Olson, but the upstairs one was available, so we rented that.

Ruby Olson had a little baby so that worked out well. However, we were both low on cash. There was a tuna fish canning plant near by so we decided that she would take the morning shift and I would take the afternoon, and we would watch each other's children. This allowed us to make some extra cash, which we needed.

Elaine loved to play with the baby, so that worked out well. Sometime, our sailors would come home, so we all looked forward to the evening, but were disappointed many times when they were overseas or out on the ocean, coming and going. Ruby always made a delicious supper. She loved to cook.

The ladies who worked in the tuna fish canning factory had to wear white clothes, but by the day's end they had become quite soiled and we smelled!! So, we had to sit in the back of the bus.

One evening I spied my sailor get on the bus, and he sat down in the front row. When the bus stopped we all got off - and Al started running toward our apartment. I finally caught up to him, and when he saw me in my fish apparel he was very "shocked." But, I explained that we needed the money and had taken turns working in the fish factory. Of course, he understood.

I remember he received $150 in Navy pay, and Elaine and I together received $80.

Life in World War II

I was on the farm, in the house wiping up the kitchen floor, alone at the time, when the mailman drove up to our farm home.

This was unusual, but he carried a special government letter, which was like a telegram. The mailman was worried it was a serious message concerning a serviceman, my husband, in the war.

He stood by me when I opened it - and it was from Al. "Our ship will come into the Oakland San Francisco area within a week. I will meet you there. Bring Elaine!"

He knew I had a relative there and that he had friends there, the Lembkes. Herb had been a shop teacher in Litchfield and he and Al had become friends through our store.

I called around for train schedules. No civilian could get reservations, only service men. But, the depot agent in Kimball found a way we might get on a troop train coming to the Minneapolis depot very soon.

How were we to manage to get to Minneapolis and on that train? I could qualify as a Navy man's wife. I called Uncle Peter and he responded that he would take me to the boarding station in Minneapolis. I hurriedly packed two suitcases - one for me and one for Elaine.

My parents were upset, but they realized I had to go. Uncle Peter got us through the Minneapolis traffic and to the area where servicemen were embarking to go off to war. We tried, but there was a never-ending line. One of the service men, who introduced himself as Jimmy, saw my predicament and stopped and stated, "You will not be able to get on this train unless you are the wife of a serviceman."

I retorted in tears, "My husband is in the Navy and he sent me a telegram instructing me to meet him in Oakland. The ship he is on carries servicemen in the battle zone!"

He said, "Well, I will tell them you are my wife and this is our little girl."

I was reluctant, but Elaine said, "He looks all right, and we need to meet daddy!"

That did it, and Jimmy got us on the train heading toward Oakland and San Francisco.

When we started to converse after we got settled in the train seats, Jimmy told us his sad story. "I left my wife and four children at home, I realized you wanted to meet someone special so I decided to ask you to come!" Elaine and I were both pleased. We were on the train headed for the service men's stop near Oakland-San Francisco.

The porter brought us food. Elaine had a front seat alone, as the porter was understanding and gave up his seat. He said he very seldom used it, but it was very good of him to give her a place to play. Jimmy and I and another person sat behind her.

The train rolled on rapidly until it came to a sudden jolting stop! It stopped dead on the tracks in a small town - Green River, Wyoming. The servicemen got out and were off for sometime.

When they returned, they had raided the grocery stores and liquor stores and brought back food and liquor. They drank as they made sandwiches for us. We were hungry so we ate their stolen food. It was then that one of the ladies blew a whistle she carried and said, "Gentlemen, you are looking at the wife of a general. He is expecting me in the Oakland-San Francisco stop!" They got the message!!!

The next stop for the Navy recruits was San Francisco, so I was certain that we could stay with my cousin, Lavonne. That didn't work out as my cousin was a busy lady and had other plans evidently.

However, I needn't have been concerned. Al had notified Herb and Evelyn Lembke that the ship was coming ashore and they met him. Then, they had found out what train Elaine and I were on and, when the troop train pulled to a stop near San Francisco, they were there to meet us. We couldn't believe it! We were covered with dust from head to toe. We didn't care - we were together as a family for a short time. The Lembkes were wonderful! They did everything to make us comfortable.

Al brought his little girl into the bathroom and gave her a bath, wrapped her in a towel and found her clothes so she could dress herself. When we sat down to eat she wanted to sit as near her daddy as possible. After the meal he put her to bed. We were exhausted from the traveling experience and retired shortly.

The Lembkes were gracious hosts., Evelyn served home-cooked meals and took us for rides, but mostly allowed us time to be a family together again for a short time.

Al was scheduled to be aboard ship so we drove as near as we could to the troops boarding area. He left in a P.T. boat, again headed for the troop ship. We had parted with tears again! However, we never forgot our wonderful friends, Herb and Evelyn Lembke.

A Bowl to Remember

When my grandfather, Iver Justeson., came to America, the land from Dassel through the North Kingston area was covered with trees. He homesteaded or purchased a piece of property in the North Kingston area.

He sawed down trees on the land with help from his 14 year old son John, my father. Then he built a log house and my grandmother, Christina and the rest of the family moved from her relatives in Dassel into the log house. My grandmother was delighted - she had her own home.

As time went on, they acquired animals and necessities gradually, but in order to supplement their income, they sawed down more trees and made smaller wood chunks that could be sold for fuel to heat homes.

They loaded the sled with wood and sent my father to Litchfield to sell the wood. Grandmother sent sandwiches along, but he was allowed a nickel to spend for a hot drink.

My father was quite an aggressive salesman and managed to develop places to sell his loads of wood.

On one of these trips, by sled to Litchfield, he looked in a store window and saw a beautiful bowl. It was priced $1.50.

He said to himself, "My mother hasn't had anything beautiful since she came from Sweden - and she has worked so hard!"

He didn't hesitate, he spent the $1.50 that he had received for the sled full of wood and brought the bowl home all wrapped in a pretty package.

When he arrived home his mother Christine inquired, "Where is the money, John?"

He gave her the package and while she was opening it, he said, "Mon Mor (mother), you have worked so hard I spent all the money on this gift for you."

Then grandmother sat down, placed her head on the table and started to cry as she opened the gift.

My father thought she was crying because he had spent the money for the gift, but she said, "You are a good boy, John. Do they have anymore of these dishes?"

He assured her that there were sauce dishes that matched the bowl and a water pitcher and glasses, too.

She then replied, "I'll save my egg money so you can buy the sauce dishes and other dishes later!"

In time, more custard glass dishes were acquired and placed in a china closet at Grandma's house. They were seldom used, but were a great source of pride for grandmother.

Before my grandmother passed away, she gave the glassware to my mother, who packed them carefully in an egg case and placed them in a storage area in our home. She said to me, "You can have these dishes, I have too much food preparation around this kitchen, so they might get broken!"

When I married Al she presented me with the egg case containing the custard glass saying, "Of course you will give it to your daughter (Elaine), and she will give it to one of her sons. Some things should remain in the family forever! It <u>can not be sold</u> It must be passed from generation to generation."

We have no assurances that this will happen. There could be a fire, severe storm or other sorts of disasters.

In the meantime, we can cherish the memory that the article has to tell. I have written the story of the custard glass, passed on to me by my mother, and placed it in the custard glass sugar bowl with a cover.

A Place to Remember - Lake Ripley

We drove around the lake when we were tired - after work, before we went home - and felt better!

This is the lake, where my daughter, Elaine, and her friend Joan Langseth, (age 14 years old) decided to swim across the lake, causing much concern.

Their fathers Al Hummel and Jens Langseth responded quickly when summoned. They quickly got in a rowboat and followed them.

The girls almost made it to the opposite shore - but were grateful that their fathers were there in a boat to assist them if needed.

This is the lake, that during one dry season almost dried up. Everyone was concerned! The rains finally came and the water level rose again!

This is the lake, we would purposely drive out to and park on the east side to view the sunset.

This is the lake, we sat by to be consoled after visiting the cemetery across the way.

This is the lake, where we would rent a boat, but seldom caught any fish.

This is the lake, where couples would park their cars near by and enjoy a short period of making love!

Did you ever do it?

Did I do it?   I'll never tell!!

Julianne J. Johnson

This year has been one of change as Juli's family grows and moves in different directions. She has become more introspective in her writing and independent in her thinking, seeking more time to devote to writing, studying, learning and growing. "Daily God places exciting new opportunities before me, and I can't wait to see what He has for me as each new day unfolds."

Life in a Place

I have learned that it's people that make a place special. And I know this for certain now that I've lost people I've known and loved and the place where I loved them.

After my brother died, and then my dad, there was a definite sadness that stretched itself out across our farm. Like a cloud, its shadow didn't bring total darkness or complete despair, but cast a pall, a mark of imperfection that was stationary and unchanging.

I grew used to the lack of their voices, the absence of their presence, but still things were never right after that. There was an incompleteness to our lives that we were unable to fix.

When I go back home, just in my mind now because it's no longer our farm, I only see the good times, I only replay the happy moments. My senses awaken to anything I want to experience, anything at all, and it is excruciatingly vivid. I gasp in wonder at what I remember when I have one of those flashbacks, so powerful that I'm momentarily stunned.

The bird song is so familiar I can hear it anytime I want ... blackbirds "chick-chick" in the tall pines near the house, pigeons coo in the haymow, the mourning dove's sad call comes from somewhere far away in the grove. The weathervane atop the barn roof makes a rusty gate sound as it turns in the switching wind. I hear the back screen door slam shut with a "thunk," the woodpecker's rattle on the trunk of an elm, the squeak of the rope on the tire swing as I soar into the treetops, the bullfrogs in the ditch with their throaty croak making a duet with the cricket's monotonous rasp. And I always hear my dad's booming voice answered by my mom's soft soothing one, and my brothers' laughter as they wrestle in the living room.

I see random, orange daylily beds and green asparagus spears growing wild in the woods, golden bales of straw stacked in the haymow, corncribs bursting with bright yellow cobs, ruby raspberries cascading off the brambly bushes lining the driveway. Dad in his seedcorn cap is driving the tractor, my brothers are grinding feed and cleaning the barn, Mom is hanging clothes on the line.

I catch a whiff of wood smoke from a brushfire in the clearing south of the house, the rich scent of freshly turned black dirt in the field, the aroma of bacon and eggs, toast and coffee on the breakfast table, the oily stench of grease in the machine shed, the earthy smell of cattle and hay in the barn, fragrant lilacs towering in a canopy over my secret hideaway in the thicket, the green tomato vines in the garden, plump pink peonies bursting into bloom by the side of the garage, freshly cut grass as the lawn is mowed, and the smell of fragrant clover from a second cutting of hay in the alfalfa field.

All of the good things we shared there on the farm were made better by being part of a family, whole and intact, laboring together in love and oneness. Not perfect, not deliriously happy even, but not yet fragmented by change, either. In that corner of my mind where we once shared this space in time, we still live before we knew the anguish and bitter pain of premature death, accidental or deliberate. But my assurance of reunion melts the momentary sorrow of our separation and I remember that even though we are apart for now, life not shared is not life at all, and I'm grateful for the days we had together.

Bridging the Gap

"Is something wrong?"
"I don't know."
"Do you want to talk about it?"
"I don't care."
"Are you mad at me?"
"Why do you ask?"
"What did I do?"
"It doesn't matter."

For years, I never stated my true feelings. I learned early on that people often don't really want to hear what you think or feel. They want to hear what they want to hear. And I never wanted to offend anyone, put them out, be a bother, cause an altercation of any kind. I shied away from being honest. I bit my tongue a lot.

For the most part, as a child, I was surrounded by loving, caring, affirming adults. When I was criticized by someone, I'd simply avoid that someone and latch on to positive, happy, laid-back people. I have horrible memories of being attacked, physically and verbally by certain individuals, mostly in my adolescent years. It hurt at the time, and I would turn the other cheek, but in my head I was creating witty, equally insulting comebacks, picturing vicious revenge. I remember being called horrid names by older kids, abused on the playground, attacked by ugly old men, humiliated by others. Today we, thank goodness, would not tolerate injustice like this. We can't stop it, but we can, and do fix it for the moment, anyway.

I did have a stubborn streak about my beliefs and held fast to what I knew was right. This posed a few problems in my teenage years, however. I was left out of certain party circles and persecuted some, but still I held my ground.

When I got married, I still was reticent about sharing my true feelings, so I would get angry when I felt mistreated. I expected my husband to know what I wanted and needed. He did his best, but there were times when he failed miserably to fill me. When I tried to explain, in my awkwardness, what I wanted it was always "shoot the messenger" time and we would miss the mark by a long shot in solving our dilemma. As long as I was happy, we were fine. Whenever I wasn't, look out. He wasn't good at honest, problem-solving communication either.

In recent years, however, I've discovered I'm changing. I realize how wrong it is to expect people to read your mind, to expect closeness and wavelength compatibility if honesty and upfront, forthright dialogue is missing. It's impossible. I'm happy to say that now I've finally learned to tell anyone and everyone how I feel, what I think and what I want. I strive to be unselfish and fair, but I am happier than ever since I've learned to be an honest communicator.

Would this have changed the injustice of my past? I really believe it would have. You will be used and abused as long as you allow yourself to be. Is this consistent with Christian thought? Again, I believe so. We are to love our neighbor as ourselves, but it's not love to be a doormat. It's the lie of the enemy that we are not worthy and somehow deserve to be trampled.

There's a story about a young woman so distraught by all the evil and injustice in the world that she cried out to God, asking Him how he could allow so much awful stuff in the world and why didn't He do something about it? He said, "I have... I created you to love one person, one day at a time."

When I allow God's love to be what truly fills me, I am, in turn, able to love just about anyone and, with openness and honesty, work on differences in order to bridge any gaps and to develop unity in all of my relationships.

Life Journey

I entered the world, red and wrinkled
Birth date pushed ahead by an impatient doctor.
I screamed, colicky and forced into a world.
Already inhabited by a baby...
My brother, a one-year-old, needing constant surveillance.
My busy mother's arms protected him,
As my bottle was propped and I cried angrily.
Needing, craving the warmth and comfort
of my dark fluid cradle. Birthed too soon.

Yet, I grew, knob-kneed and blonde-haired.
I laughed, jumped, shrieked.
"Yo-yo," I was named. Never still a moment.
As I grew, every day I asked one question:
"Are we going anywhere today
or is anyone coming to visit?"
Always seeking fun, if it didn't come to me, I made it on my own. Mudpies, a bike ride, soaring high in the tire swing, cuddling kittens in the haymow, tag with my brothers, paper dolls in my room, singing my heart out in the treehouse.

Later, rollerskating parties, movies, sleepovers, prom dates,
A whirlwind courtship and marriage.

Halfway through my life,
in the middle of a stormy December night,

A View From The Verandah

With a single sentence, my life was forever changed.
"He's dead."
And I cried for my teenaged brother.
I cried for 5 years.

But the God of my fathers,
the great Jehovah jireh, El-Shaddai, Adoni, Elohim,
The One who knit me together in my mother's womb,
who knew me before I was born,
Picked me up.
He wiped the tears from my eyes,
took my shattered heart and,
Piece by jagged piece, put it back together again.
He smoothed the scars and replaced the heartache
with His boundless joy and peace.

Now I live to please Him ...
He caused me to see He's all I need.
And as for me and my house, we will serve the Lord,
THE MOST HIGH
MY RESTING PLACE
THE ALMIGHTY GOD
THE ONE WHO SUSTAINS ME
THE ROCK IN WHOM I TAKE REFUGE
THE SPRING OF LIVING WATER
THE STRENGTH OF MY HEART
THE HOLY ONE, THE AWESOME TRUE GOD.

I have found that down at His feet
Is the Most High Place.
And I just want to praise and thank Him
For "He took the shackles off my feet so I could dance."

Again.

Herb Life

There's a chill in the air
A bite, a sting, a nip.
Tonight frost will kiss tender leaves,
Painting white the tips of each.

Tonight this wondrously fragrant bed
Will be no more.
What I'll harvest, must come now:
Armfuls of scented stalks,
Leafy greens, spiky celadon, flaccid sage.

Life will be silenced
On this square of earth
When the sun drops;
The temperature falls,
And the cool darkness settles
Upon this bed of living balm
And it will heal no more.

In the morning,
Vibrant marigolds and zinnia heads
Will be dulled, stained ruddy and speckled
From nature's war,
Waged upon their fair heads.

But I will rejoice because
What I pulled from this treasured plot
Will fill jar after jar
Upon my pantry shelf.

Dried, leaden colors,

Dead and crumbled,
Will make my winter kettles sing
With life. Life from my garden
Revived in all of its savory splendor
In simmering pots of stew.

Making Relish

On a cool September morning,
Before the last tomatoes ripen on the vine,
Find a bucketful of green ones.
Pick about a dozen peppers
Red, green and yellow, the colors of fall

To preserve in a jar.

Gather half a dozen sweet onions, the size of your fist.
Papery skins shedding like confetti at your feet.
Then, the cabbage. Three medium heads will do.

You'll need a couple of hours now.
Washing, coring, slicing, chopping.
When the enamel pot is full, stir in a cup of sea salt.
Put the cover on and forget it till tomorrow.

Overnight, the enormous pot of vegetables
Will have relinquished their juice,
Coaxed out by a mere cup of sodium chloride.

The back hallway carries a heavy scent
of soon-to-be pickled produce.
Now comes the hard part...

A View From The Verandah

A cup at a time,
The shredded tomatoes, peppers, onions and cabbage must
be drained. Squeeze each portion by hand through a square of
cheesecloth
Extracting every trace of brine.

Now you're ready to boil it all in a syrupy blend of
Apple cider vinegar,
Brown sugar, and
Pickling spices.

Stir and sample, stir and sample.

An hour later, fully cooked, the mixture has become

Piccalilli. Green tomato relish.

Ladle the dark sauce, savory and piquant, into hot jars.

Wipe the rim and cover each jar with lids and rings.

Boil for ten minutes in a canner.

The hot water bath method.

Remove each jar
(taking care not to burn your fingers).
Place them, one by one, on a red-checkered cloth to cool.

Sigh with satisfaction as the lids "Snap!"
Sealed.

Now share with your friends
The delightful taste of
Your end-of-summer garden.

Camilla Werner Katlack

Camilla Werner Katlack was born on a farm in Rose Creek, Minnesota. Her family later moved to Meeker County where she attended a country school and then Litchfield High School. After graduation, she moved to Washington, D.C., where she worked for the F.B.I. She married Thomas Katlack, and in time, they moved back to her family farm in Meeker County. They are the parents of three sons a daughter. In Meeker County, Camilla has worked in a greenhouse, and has been a 4-H leader and a Master Gardener for the Extension Service. She joined the Litchfield Writers Group and began writing to record family history.

Remember When?

Remember when baby girls wore pink and baby boys wore blue? Boys had short hair and only girls wore earrings. All boys over the age of nine carried jackknives in their pockets. And a peeling knife in a lunchbox was for cutting an apple, tomato or cucumber. Girls had to wear dresses to school and everyone put on their best clothes to go to church.

Things were different back then. There were one-room schools, with a teacher who taught grades one through eight. There were no hot lunches. Everyone brought something to eat from home. All students had to practice penmanship, which was a series of exercises to improve your writing. Geography was a subject that included drawing maps. Large pull-down maps hung on the front wall, along with a big blackboard for working problems on. The "Pledge of Allegiance" was said every morning and songs were sung. The flag was run-up on an outside flagpole. The big kids in grades six, seven and eight could help the little kids, if they had their own work done. At noon hour, games of "Anti-I-Over the Schoolhouse," "Prisoners' Base," and "Red Rover" were played. Everyone walked to school. If a father stopped at school to pick up his children, everyone going in that direction piled-in too. Sometimes there were as many as six in the back seat and two or three in the front. There were no seat belts.

Those were the days when mothers stayed home. Monday was wash day and clothes were hung outside on lines. Clothes had to be ironed too, for wrinkle-free material had not yet been invented. Fathers had jobs and most had Sundays off. After church and a big dinner, people went visiting since there was no television. Popcorn was made in a frying pan on top of the stove and families played cards in the evenings. Most homes had coal or wood-burning heaters in the living room. This meant that the kitchen and living room were nice and warm but that very little heat got upstairs. People had feather beds and homemade quilts to keep the cold away.

Yes, things were sure different then ... and I don't think I want to go back.

Timetable to Sunrise

5:30 a.m. Just a hint of light in the sky. It is not night anymore. I can make out the trees, so dark against the white snow. So quiet--not a sound and nothing moving.

6:00 a.m. There's a light pink tinge in the east. It is much brighter there than the rest of the sky and, oh, so still. Nothing seems to move. The birds are not even up yet.

6:30 a.m. The white trail of a jet suddenly appears, without a sound, almost like magic.   Now the pink eastern sky is tinged yellow-orange, and the sky to the west has a gray-blue look. The jet trail spreads out to four times the width it was and begins to disappear. Headlights of cars punctuate the darkness and the sound of their motors breaks the quiet. People are starting to go to work. I can see their lights a mile away as they come over the hill from the east. It's light enough now that I can see plainly. The sky blushes like a ripe peach.

6:45 a.m. Deep pink now covers a large area. Suddenly, the big red sun appears. It comes up from behind the neighbor's farm-from behind the trees just above the corn crib. It is a ball of fire, a picture to paint. I can no longer look at it-it is too bright.

7:00 a.m. I take my last peek at the sun. It is full now and rising in the sky, ready to take over the day with all its power. The first bird, a hungry woodpecker, arrives. The world is awake once more.

Quilts

Squares of green and yellow, red and blue.
Squares of flowers and frogs, kittens and dogs.
Squares of checks and stripes, dots and plaids.
Lap robes and baby quilts, coverlets and pillows.

All to be made with a snip of a scissors,
A stitch of thread, a filler so soft, a matching back;
Tied or quilted;
To give away or to sell
To a friend or a stranger.
Making someone
Warm and cozy,
Peaceful and sleepy,
Content and dreamy,
Wrapped
In a quilt
Of love.

Grandmother

The stone is large and made of gray granite. It is cold and impersonal. But here lie family members who once walked and talked, worked and danced, ate and slept. How I wish you had left a record for me to read, but I can only imagine most of your story.

"Hello Grandmother! What a brave person you were to leave your home and come to a world that you had only heard about ... to leave all your friends for what would be a new life in a strange land."

"Yes, that was hard--but the worst part was crossing the ocean. A bad storm shook the ship and put it back many miles.

We thought all would be lost. My sister said she would like to go back for a visit, if they would build a bridge."

"Did your family have a large farm in Germany? And did you have any pets?"

"Our farm was only 40 acres. The land was out from town, with the house and barn in town. The barn was attached to the house. Every day, it had to be swept-out and the cows taken out to pasture. We had a cat to keep down the mouse population--gave it to a friend before we left."

"I hear you found a new pet cat here in America."

"Oh, you mean the big beautiful black one with the white stripe down its back. We were so happy when that cat came to the barn. It drank milk from a bowl, but we could not pet it. Then, a neighbor came over and said we had better kill it as it was a skunk and would eat the chickens. We did so hate to do that, but the neighbor came the next day with a cat from his farm for us."

"Did you have many boyfriends? And how did you come to marry Grandfather?"

"There were several other families here from our part of Germany--so we soon had a circle of friends. There were two boys who were special. Father preferred Michael, so he became my husband."

"How did you come to move to Litchfield?"

"Michael had a brother who lived there, and there was this 80 acre farm for sale at a good price. It even had a small frame house on it, so we did not have to live in a log cabin."

"You had a large family to feed and care for in a small house. That must have been hard." "Seven children was not so large a family in our day. We did not get rich, but always had enough to eat and clothes to put on our backs. By knitting our socks and mittens, and sewing our shirts and dresses, we got by. Most of our children went out to work at an early age. I spent all my married life on that farm. It was home."

Rest on, Grandmother, under your quilt of grass. You had a hard life--and then again, maybe only hard by our standards.

Could I do what she did? Maybe so ... as I too have some of that blood running through my veins.

Busy Day

The day is warm,
The sun is out,
And Spring is here
Without a doubt.
Things to do-
There's quite a list:
Lawns to rake;
Pick up the sticks;
Uncover flowers;
Plant a tree;
Dig out the weeds ...
Now let me see ...
Plow the garden;
Plant the seeds;
Water plants ...
Oh goodness me! ...
Put back the rake-
The shovel too.
A storm is coming.
It's starting to brew.

Patrik Mattsson

Patrik Mattsson is a retired psychologist, 78 years of age. He has been a member of the Litchfield Area Writers Group since 1990, but, due to impairment caused by Parkinson's and scoliosis, has not been able to attend monthly meetings for a year or so. He is now attempting to write his stories in poetry form.

My Random Family

I am Swedish
I am German
I am English
I am French
I am my family

Most of us lived long, long ago,
Have used up our brief time as pulsing,
Struggling, living creatures,
Have returned to the dust from which we came.

The genes of my many ancestors are not lost, however.
They were passed on to their children
And grandchildren and all offspring that followed
Were altered by extraterrestrial radiation,
Creating individual differences,
Yet allowing similarities within family groups.

That is why I do not look like Neanderthal man,
Although he is one of my relatives.

A View From The Verandah

What I actually look like is based upon what parts
Of the combined gene pool of my parents
Imprinted themselves on me at the moment of
My conception. Random, random, random.
It staggers me to think
How accidental the "I" in all of us started:
I could easily have been born a woman,
Or have developed a different personality than I have.
Random, random.

For seventeen years I spoke Swedish daily,
My father's tongue, before I left my Swedish family
To settle in America.
I like the Swedish language, because it carries
The emotions of my youth.
When I speak that old language with those
Who also know it, I feel livelier, stronger and
Younger.

But who we are and what we speak
Is mostly left to chance, as it was for me.
If I had grown up in a different family,
I may have known myself as Alex or even Kuckeli-muck!
(Actually the name of my father's cat.)
What crazy names parents can give their children!
I knew an Indian boy whose first name was Anderson!
Random, random!

My place in the timetable of family events,
Random as they were, could have made me 28 now
Instead of 78, and that would be nice.
But I am 78 and live in constant awareness of
My disabilities, and all the support from
Family and friends cannot change that.

A View From The Verandah

I am in the winter of my life, have used up
Most of my allotted days, and existence,
As I have known it, will soon come to an end.
And I don't know if anything will come after that.
And just as this poem will end without any explanations,
My days will likewise end.

Corrine Blikstad Nelson

Born, raised, educated and a life long resident of the state of Minnesota has been a gift I treasure. It is a life tied together in faith, love, great endurance, sacrifice, victories, education, and blessings. There are many positives in writing one's way into retirement. It has helped me to crystallize, recall, and qualify life's values as I see my thoughts written down. My golden age of opportunity is here. Writing is fun, writing is therapy, and it is like a game or puzzle I play with myself. All I need is paper and pencil and energy with discipline and a clear mind. But writing becomes hard work when you want to present it in words that make sense to the reader. May I pass on to family and friends the ability to see our own comic fallibility and enjoy a quality of life that gives tranquility without complacency because of our faith which is much larger than ourselves.

A Lite Candle

Once upon a time I as a small child envisioned a house which I could call my perfect home. It never entered my mind the magic of how it would someday come.

Pictures were cut from catalogs and books, newspapers or magazines. I drew pictures of castles and colored them in a rainbow of colors. With friends I created houses in fields of tall grasses. We would put down a rug, blanket or a wood board, which would press down the grass and create a room. We would soon have a running maze of rooms as our house grew and grew.

A View From The Verandah

Then there were the warm summer days by the lakeshore. We built castles in the sand with one castle bigger than the other. In winter, we built igloos and other ice houses which gave us the feeling of seclusion, togetherness, and a warm feeling of home. Under the Christmas tree one year, I received a dollhouse full of furniture. I would arrange, re-arrange and even ended up coloring the walls. Family and friends built up my self-esteem by compliments that made me want for more and more. More furniture, more people, more pets, more, more. The cost and interest of playhouses soon became prohibited, and I graduated onto graph paper and drawing or using paper cut-outs. I drew large halls and stairways where walls could be covered with famous art works like that of Rembrandt, Picasso or Michelangelo. There would then be a drawing room, music room, library, dining room, kitchen, living room, game room, laundry and sewing room, or whatever my mind could wish for. In my drawings, I could create everything of my heart's desire. This was a time in my life I observed from the world around me, reading of fairy stories, princes, and kings who seemed to live in a perfect world. Enjoy, laugh, and the world laughs with you. Even during my years in college and graduate school, there was always a rosy lining. Climb higher, the best is yet to come. Think big, there is always room at the top. So I pushed, climbed, laughed and enjoyed, always dreaming to arrive and live in my perfect castle of many rooms.

Then came the day of my first job. I was being paid for a day's work of teaching in a public school. I thought I was on the road to being rich, but as I was paid, I spent and gave and, when the end of my first year came, I had no money to buy a castle or even pay down on one. So I taught another year and lo and behold, I fell in love, and together we could build a one-story house, three bedrooms, and living/dining combination, kitchen and bath. So my dreams were squeezed and pushed and I lost the feel of a castle. I adjusted, but kept on dreaming and drawing plans. In a few years, we made it into a larger house, more rooms, more stuff. Always trying to create an illusion of grandeur. I adjusted again but kept on dreaming of walls filled with art work. I painted pictures, painted china, sewed, papered, painted, gardened and kept house. I continued to work at teaching school for 35 years. During this time, I also served in many organizations - community, church, county and state. I worked, enjoyed, laughed, cried and raised a family of two plus my husband. I adjusted again but kept on dreaming. The day soon came to what they call retirement years. The push was still on. The song and verse rang through my mind, "work for the night cometh."

When I relax, I usually like to light a fragrant candle and sit in my favorite chair and read. It is then I have time to dream, create and live in a world of my own liking of castles, rooms, art, love, beauty, peace, serenity and freedom. One day in this quiet spot, I caught a whiff of something wrong. I hurried into the kitchen only to find a strong wind had blown through my kitchen window and had blown the tablecloth over the lit candle. Flames hit the ceiling, burning the tablecloth and parts of the cloth had fallen down on the carpet and were burning. In a state of panic, I grabbed the salt, towels and what I could to smother the flames. But the flames were too widespread by this time.

Today, as I look back on that frightful day, I picture an ending which tells me the truth of what could have easily been the result of that fire. Thank God, this ending is not true, but the lesson taught to me will live forever. Recalling that day, I imagined the ending which could have been.

The fire was spreading rapidly. I called 911, I seemed to lose my ability to speak or think. In a daze, I grabbed my Bible on the shelf nearby and ran out the front door. By this time, smoke was billowing all around me. The firemen and rescue squad were running around. I was quickly put into the ambulance and rushed to the hospital for smoke inhalation and burns. Here I stayed for the night and into the next day. When I returned home to my created castle, I saw only myself clutching my Bible. All my castle building was now nothing, just nothing but ash.

Who am I? A living breathing human being with a Bible in my hand. Once upon a time as an old woman I envisioned, not a candle made by hand sending fragrance around, but I as a living soul to give light and fragrance from the message in the book that I hold. When this truth enters the human heart, it leads to the castles which are eternal, which no mind could imagine. This was the fire that lit the candle to the eternal castle, which we call home.

Diamonds In Water

When asked, what was your most nostalgic and memorable vacation taken as a child, I did not have to think twice. The picture has emerged in my mind often and especially when I want to relax, relieve tension or send myself into a fairy land of thought. What quality does this vacation have which creates these strong and exciting moments in my life? It is found in the simple yet complex properties of water. When water is hit by sunlight, it propels numerous diamonds to sparkle in the observer's eyes. My most memorable vacations were spent with my family and seeing the many diamonds found in Crystal Lyda Lake.

This lake was northeast of Pelican Rapids, Minnesota. Pelican was my mother's home town and where I was born. My grandfather owned and operated one of the first funeral and furniture businesses in this area. This was then a territory which reached from Detroit Lakes to Fergus Falls, where now there are many funeral homes and furniture stores dotting that area. My mothers mother, or my grandmother's name, along with her parent's names, appear on a plaque in the Triangular Park on the north end of Pelican as the first white people to settle in this part of Minnesota. Pelican was, and still is, blessed with rich soil, beautiful trees, flowers, hills, peaks, and surrounded by many lakes where one finds the Diamonds in Water.

We always stayed on the east shore of Crystal Lyda. A few doors from our cabin, mother's sister, Clara and her husband Rev. Olaf Bratten and seven children stayed in a larger cabin which was owned by one of Grandpa's good friends. Next door to our cabin, was another minister's family with three children. My sister and I seemed to have fun from morning to night playing with all the children. Once we all crossed the little gravel road going by our cottages and placed blankets, paper boxes or boards into long grass and created a play house. It was a maze of fun. I remember we brought lunch to our grass house and enjoyed a meal absent of adults. The shore line of the lake consisted of a wide area of white sand in which we played by the hour creating castles, roads, and lakes and rivers which would run into the lake. We gathered branches, flowers, and weeds and planted around our buildings. On rainy days, we told stories or put on plays. The greatest fun came in the water. We would run or jump into the lake, swim, have water fights and just splash around creating the million sparkles of diamonds. We saw the diamonds in the moving water and waves. We saw them when we went gliding in our wooden boat over sunfish weeds, dropping our anchor with a splash then feeling when it hit bottom. We each had a small piece of wood with a fish line and hook wound on it. We put our worms on, which we had dug in the woods behind the cottages. We felt the fish bite and enjoyed seeing the diamonds of water around the fish as we pulled it into the boat. What a magic wonder to look over the edge of the boat and into the clear sparkling water and see the various colors of vegetation and, if we looked close, we could see fish weaving in and out between the leaves.

We carried a pail to the pump to get water for drinking, cleaning and washing. There was the kerosene stove, the sparsely furnished cabin with the bare necessities and our trips to the outhouse with its Sears Roebuck catalog or peach wrappers, all pale in comparison to the spirit created in me with Diamonds in Water.

The vacations of my childhood at Crystal Lyda Lake gave to me joy, thrills, and the constant security found in a loving family. May the constant excitement, transparent emotions, empowered spirit be received by all as they see the DIAMONDS IN WATER.

Rare Treasure

Observing the skylines of most large cities, we see many of the tallest buildings are trade centers, insurance, or bank places. Within these buildings, people have jobs of filing, sorting, storing, selling and taking great care of what this world holds so dear. Be it gems, jewels, gold, silver, land or other investments which man strives to possess. When you enter these buildings there is a feeling of space, control and often being unapproachable. They are built with the finest of materials and architectural design. This greatness gives a desire for possession and the presence of mind to share in this great treasure.

Observing people in the market places around the world, we see individuals searching for something rare and special and many are bound in the urge to collect precious and valued artifacts which they may add to their store of treasures. These items may vary with desire such as pictures, jewelry, gems, art work, land, buildings, boats and always for more and more power, possession or self worth.

From early childhood, we all have been busy with learning how to live, how to receive, express ourselves, learning to crawl, walk, run, sing, skip, and hop. Then there are the learning skills such as reading, writing, playing. Each skill building upon another. From nursery school to preschool, middle school, high school, college and graduate school, the push goes on. These things are all good and needed for our achievement of success. With this pressure, we are always looking for what we treasure and our own happiness. Many times our wants may surpass our needs or the ability to reach.

In the rush, noise and clamor around us, our minds may lose track of our true values of what we truly treasure. The rarest of all treasures is seldom found. It is exceptional, yet scarce, and few and far between seems to be found. Yet, this rare treasure is within each person's grasp. We have a pointer in the little verse, which goes, "Where your treasure is there will your heart be also." Yes, the rarest of all treasures is found in the heart. Also, rare is the person who has enjoyed this treasure for a lifetime. Search with all your heart and you shall find this rare treasure burning in your heart. To find this treasure an individual must become quiet so the mind can reach and see this great need. The rare treasure is to find true love, true love of companionship, true love of self, true love of work. This love is pure as crystal, sharp as a diamond, genuine, perfect, complete, giving, renewing, sustaining, and creating. It is life itself, for God is love. "Faith, hope, love and the greatest is love. Love they neighbor as thy self." True love is a rare treasure and a wealth stored not in skylines, buildings or material things, but a Rare Treasure of Love found the human heart.

Boy Next Door

Slow as molasses in January
Is said of the boy next door
As he mowed the grass then to tarry
At the garden gate at four.

With a day's work soon ended
And time for fun and banter
A creative spark his min now needed
The place where no other may enter.

He slowly sauntered homeward bound
Then stopped to watch boys playing ball.
One, two, three, You're out was the sound
Thoughts of ball, then school, then fall.

So he continued toward home
Where he was met with smiles of love
Dearer than all else where he would roam
Now a welcomed rest under the rafters above.

Fall came and squirrels their nuts were stacking.
Cool breezes blew and leaves turned golden brown.
The boy next door took to raking
With the same slow motions up and down.

He raked; he carried, and burnt the leaves,
Then watched the flames to the last flicker
And counted the many barren trees
As cold temperature made molasses thicker.

With chill in the air soon to bring snow

Covering the land with more work to do.
He would then shovel as the wind did blow
In his same slow sluggish motion too.

Through the long winter days he pondered
To make mowing, raking, shoveling merry
With a push button could be remote controlled
This was the boy slow as molasses in January.

The Right Will Prevail

History always teaches us a lesson. In our human struggle to survive with ever-present selfishness, man has a need for politics and the law. When we study and observe the past, one truth rises to the top and that is, "The right will prevail." When we look at the present, it many times gets difficult to believe, but when we lengthen out the time span, the picture becomes clearer.

Back in the 1950's, the country school enrollment had become smaller and smaller and so, closing up of school districts was in full swing in our West Central Minnesota area. A country school would close and then join in with the nearest town school, which had both grade and high school. In the fall of 1950, I started my first year of teaching in a small town which had just begun to receive students from some of these rural schools. It was exciting to be a part of this intermingling of different ways of working together.

Outside the classrooms other feelings and struggles were happening. In one of the country schools, there was left an old bell in the storage room, which no one seemed to notice. One day Mr. Spark came to the town school board and wanted to donate a bell to the town school. He had his name put on the bell and it was installed on a nice cement slab outside of the town school in front of my class room window. Everyone was happy and thanked Mr. Spark for the mighty fine, neighborly gesture.

The day soon came when Mr. Spark's school district found the need to close the school and send their children to the town school. In the clearing out of school supplies and equipment someone noticed the bell was missing. After much searching, it was found out that Mr. Spark had taken the bell from the school and had given it to the town school with his name on the bell. Mr. Spark's school board met and voted they would donate the bell to the town school, but said that Mr. Spark's name must be taken off.

One day, as I was looking out my classroom window, I noticed the bell was removed from its resting-place. A few weeks later, it was placed back on the cement slab, the same as before, but with the name missing. A mark still remains where the name was taken off. Everyone seemed happy and satisfied except, I would suppose, Mr. Spark. But, in the long run of history, I hope even he will be thankful that the RIGHT WILL PREVAIL.

Grove City Women's Club - A Treasure

The women of this West Central town, Grove City Minnesota, have joined their hands and spirit together for over 50 years to assist in helping build a beautiful, neat and orderly community for people to live. Their efforts may be hidden treasures, which the searching eye can quickly see and appreciate. There are many projects and values of this treasure found throughout the community.

On a beautiful September day, over 50 years ago, I had my first sight of the town of Grove City. I had no realization of what an effect a Women's Club such as this would have on my life. Green and apprehensive, yet self-assured, I felt ready to start my first year of teaching Home Economics, Girl's Physical Education, and speech in the local high school. There were five first year teachers in the school system that year. We quickly developed a close camaraderie and enjoyed finding what this town had to offer. It offered three eating places, three grocery stores, a drug store, and meat market. There were two hardware stores, beauty and barbershops, a pool hall, doctor, dentist, and lawyer's offices. Plus a bank, a post office, a creamery, two grain elevators, two car dealerships and train or bus service enabling us to go and come within the same day to far away places like Willmar, Minneapolis, St. Paul, or Litchfield. Most first year teachers did not have cars and so trains, busses, and friends were very important.

Within a few weeks of teaching, I found out a group of area Women met in the Home Economics room once a month, right after my last class was dismissed. They kindly asked me to join them and expected me to become a member. From that day to the present, I have continued to learn the importance of women working together to establish a healthy energetic community. Being a member you are committed to serve others, but in so doing, you see and experience the joys of membership. Even when one feels like throwing in the towel, you soon learn that those difficult times are sometimes the greatest joy of learning. One of the great benefits of this club is that it is open to membership to all women of the Grove City area. They read their Creed at the eight regular meetings they have each year. This Creed ends with these words; "We strive to touch and to know the real common women's heart of us all. " To grow, learn, and serve the club throughout the years has had many projects such as: bake sales, house tours, beef stew dinners, rummage sales, fairs, political rallies, concerts, talent shows, garden shows, planting of trees, and many others which creative women develop. Throughout the year, there are a few committee meetings. It is here one quickly learns the women's hearts, and to listen, to follow and lead for the enjoyment of the group. I would like to share with you the last committee meeting I was on which turned out to be hilarious, amusing and very comical. The club had voted that this year the officers should go to a wholesale supply house and purchase some supplies for the South Grove Community Room. We were given a range of money we could spend. It was decided to go to St. Cloud, take a van and ask my husband to drive. Little did he know, the many conflicting directions he would be given on this trip. As we started out on a beautiful, sunny day, we noticed some of the van windows needed cleaning; our driver had turned on the heat and not the air conditioning. Could we have a little more air, look over there, look here. I forgot the directions to the wholesale store but I have been there so many times we just cannot miss. Turn right at the next stop. Oh no, we must have taken the wrong road. I don't seem to recognize these stones. We must be on the wrong street. Back and forth we went and soon we had traveled the entire length of the main Business Street. All of sudden our driver stopped the van and left to go find directions. These directions led to another dead end and then another dead end. We then secured a phone directory. Finally, we found the right place where we were to look and buy the supplies. The four officers of the club and our driver entered the front door. In no time, we seemed to go each in a different direction. After some time, we found each other and managed to pull it together after much discussion on color, price and size. Everything decided, we were ready to go. By this time, we had lost our driver, so the four officers asked and looked for him and finally were told he was in the business office. Our van was packed with our purchases and we were ready to leave. All agreed it was time to eat a noon lunch. Where shall we go? There was a period of silence and then one said a place, almost at the same time there came two other suggestions. Our driver took the first one he heard. Where are we going? This is the wrong way. We now found we had to go around several blocks and soon came right back to the first choice. We need to go that way, to which our driver followed the best he could. In so doing, we came by a restaurant which one of the women said she had been to with friends many times. We parked here, only to hear another say, this is too ordinary." We drove on laughing and wondering if St. Cloud had a perfect place for Grove City Women's officers to eat. We drove on sharing our ideas of what we wanted, such as a clean place, good food, air-conditioning, good service, ice water and linen napkins. We became fouled up on one-way streets and difficult parking entrances. We soon came to a choice; turn left and go home or turn right and look for the right place to eat. We agreed to turn right, which took us the long way around and back to our final choice, only to find out we were on the west side of the building where there was no entrance and we needed to get to the east side. To get there, we needed to go around several more blocks. So around we went, passing the first choice again and then finding our way to the final choice. This met with our expectations and the meal was enjoyed by all. After eating, it was decided to go back to Grove City another way, which would bring us by a town known for its good bakery. Unknown to us, we ended up in road construction. We finally had finished our purchases at the bakery and one of our members said there was a wonderful restaurant where they serve delicious pies at the end of this street. To get to the end of the street, we lost some of our group as we passed the gift shops. We waited until we were all together before entering this restaurant. There were few people here, but a waitress seated us at a beautiful table by the window. When ordering, we found out they only serve dinners. We excused ourselves and quietly left by the front door. Back in the van and on our way, it was said we would be going by a great place for pies in one of the towns we would soon be coming to. The cafe was in the center of this town. We turned and drove down main street only to find we came into a mob of people and no place to park as they were having a special town festival. Looking for a way to leave, we found an alley road only to find ourselves in the middle of the caravan. We now found we could not back out or go forward but we could turn down another alley road. To everyone's relief we were out. By this time, we all felt the need for a relaxed lunch. We found one outside of town at a good sized cafe with air-conditioning. Surprises were still to come but, by now, we were well-insulated for whatever comes. It was good to finally face each other around the table and laugh and joke about our day's activity. We had now spent six hours for the joy and satisfaction of being a member of a wonderful club, which serves our community. We realized that it is the many little hidden treasures of being a member of Grove City Women's Club, which brings pleasure to all of us.

Independence Day

As a child living in rural Minnesota in the thirties, I remember with fondness the watermelon eaten at the 4th of July picnics. The succulent joy of biting into the triangular cut slice of juicy red watermelon, letting the juice run down your face and then spitting the black seeds upon the ground. Some of the children made a game out of how far they could spit the seeds.

Today, as a retired American citizen, I am overwhelmed and struck with wonder and astonished at how even the simple juicy, red watermelon fits into the celebration of the 4th of July, American Independence Day. This small seed we spit out onto the ground, when influenced by sunshine and rain gathers 200,000 times its own weight. It forces that enormous weight through a tiny stem and builds a watermelon. On the outside is a covering of green, under which a white rind forms around a juicy, red pulp carrying black seeds. These black seeds are capable of doing that same work over again. Here we are given two colors of this days celebration, the white rind covering is a symbol of purity which overall covers the red loyalty and strength with a fluid to our spirits to fight for truth and freedom. All that is left is the blue color found in the sky above. This is the truth and honesty found in the hearts of our people. Until we can explain such a little thing as a watermelon, we ought not to be absolutely sure about our wisdom. This is the message taught to me as I study the miracle and phenomenon of the development of our spectacular country which has stood for freedom throughout the world. We as a people rise to sing, "My country 'tis of thee, sweet land of liberty, let freedom ring.".

In public school class rooms, at every important national meeting, we rise to pledge allegiance to the red, white and blue which are the colors of our flag. The original author of the pledge was Francis Bellamy, who was born at Mount Morris, New York, May 18, 1855 and died August 28, 1931. He was ordained in 1879 at the Baptist church in Little Falls, New York. The pledge he wrote was first used at the dedication of the World's Fair in Chicago on October 21, 1882, the 400" anniversary of the discovery of America, and has been recited from that day to this. Rev. Bellamy's original wording was altered slightly by the First and Second National Flag Conferences in 1823 and 1924 and his work was officially designated as the Pledge of Allegiance to the Flag by Public Law 287, approved by the 79th Congress, on December 28, 1945. On June 14, 1954 Flag Day, President Dwight D. Eisenhower signed into law House Joint Resolution 243, introduced by Representative Louis C. Rabaut of Michigan, which added to the Pledge of Allegiance the compelling and meaningful words "under God."

PLEDGE OF ALLEGIANCE

I pledge allegiance to the flag
of the United States of America
and to the Republic for which it stands,
one Nation, under God, indivisible,
with liberty and justice for all.

This flag, to which we raise and pledge on the 4th of July, is the same flag we honor our service personnel who are now serving our country and those honorably discharged or that have passed away. The Stars and Stripes or Star Spangled Banner is a symbol of the thing we treasure most, freedom. Freedom of speech, politics and religion. May we not take this for granted. It is a gift we all need to guard and protect. We must remember that freedom of religion is the basic freedom for, without it, the others would never be realized. Take for example, countries where there is no religious freedom and you will find the other freedoms missing. We owe our flag and what it stand for the greatest respect and reverence.

So that I will not forget and that you may know, I would add an interesting note of information found in the American Colonel, "History of our Flag." We read that the "Raven Flag of the Vikings" was the first flag to float over the American continent. Whatever we may understand about the Vikings, we see today the places that now stand for freedom. The pilgrims came to this country for freedom. For this freedom we all need to say, as Daniel Webster said some 150 years ago, "Thank God I am an American. May we continue as free citizens and not as subjects. If it were not for yesterday's sacrifices, we could still be savages in the jungle. Our civilization, institutions are largely built by the generations, which have passed on."

On Independence Day, as the band strikes the tune "Stars and Stripes Forever" and as voices sing, "Oh say can you see" what so proudly we hailed - broad stripes and bright stars through the perilous fight -- Our flag is still there -- O'er the Land of the free, and the home of the brave. As the fire works bang, as the sparklers light the sky, as music swells I feel the juice of that watermelon run down my cheek creating a seed in my heart to force that enormous weight through a tiny stem or vessel and build that great gift to every soul. The gift of the value to be free and one's responsibility to protect America's Independence Day. Thanks for the 4th of July watermelon.

William E. Peltier

William E. Peltier is married and has three daughters. He is a pharmacist. Bill's hobbies include participation in a writers group, golfing, reading, running, theatre, and spending time with his grandchildren. "I am old enough and wise enough to know the answer, but it seems I have forgotten the question." As I have grown older, I have come to realize the light at the end of the tunnel is sometimes a reflection of the past.

A Night at the Casino

I've had some crazy times and done unusual things with some mighty curious people in my day but never anything like last weekend. Man I tell you, who ever woulda' thought I'd be playin' cards, pullin' slots and shakin' dice with one of the world's really cool dictators. Yeah, it's the truth, I swear, so help me God, on my mother's grave.

It all started when the wife told me to get lost again, so I headed for Luckypot Junction to see what I could see and if nothin' else have a good meal for a change. The wife has a lot of faults, lousy cookin' is just one of them. I drove down in my '79 Ford pickup cuz the wife had the keys to the '85 Plymouth van. The tires are really bad and so are the brakes, but it's only about 70 miles, so I figured I could make it there okay, maybe sleep in the truck. I thought about stayin' with my brother-in-law Ernie but then I remembered he was in jail in Leon County for somethin' or other.

Anyway, I pulled into the parkin' lot about 8:00 p.m. Friday night. I parked way over on the west side so maybe the cops wouldn't see the license tabs on the truck were a year old. I gets out, see, and I'm parked right next to this big humongous black limo with dark windows so you can't see in. So I think, hey, maybe this is a high roller who don't wanna attract any attention. Yuh never know who or what yur gonna find out here in the boonies. I could tell yuh some real stories pardner.

Well, a guy with one-a-them bath towels wrapped around his head (they call it a turbine) gets out of the limo and motions for me to come over, which I do. He says his boss is real shy and doesn't know anybody around here so maybe I could show him around the casino, maybe have dinner and see a show. The guy with the turbine on his noggin tells me his name is Ali Maka, and says his boss can make it worth my while. In fact he might even pick up the tab for some slots or maybe a little blackjack. So who am I to refuse to help a neighbor in need? So I say's, "Sure, tell your boss to step out of the car and we will proceed to remove a few dollars from one of Minnesota's better-known tribes."

Well, Ali Maka (I don't think that was his real name) opens the door and bows as this big bruiser wearing a camouflage military uniform with a black berret on his bean steps out. He's got a black mustache too like some of those guys you see in movies blowin' up buildings and stuff. I can hear giggling from inside the limo, which I can tell, is female, so Ali's boss ain't exactly been lonely. Know what I mean? I think they been smokin' some of that stuff that grows in Afghanistan, too. The inside of the limo smelled real funny. One whiff made me a little light-headed. Know what I mean?

Anyway, Ali introduces this bozo as Mr. Hakim, and says Mr. Hakim would like me to call him Ike. So I says, "As long as you're buyin', Ike, I'll call you anything you want." Ali goes to the trunk of the car, opens it and it's full of one hundred-dollar bills. Ike grabs a couple of fistfuls and stuffs 'em in his pockets. Well, we go in to the casino, see, and right off I see a few of my pals are there because they ain't gettin' along too well with their wives, either. I introduce them to "Ike." I tell them he's an old friend from my army days. He don't speak too good American, I tell them, but he's a good guy with lots of dough. My pals don't care about languages; money speaks real clear to them. They brighten-up real quick.

Well, we got a bunch of quarters from the cashier and start playing the quarter slots. Pretty soon Ike starts winnin' like crazy. Bell are ringin', whistles blowin,' quarters layin' all over the floor. Ike starts jumpin' up and down, yellin' somethin' in some language 1 never heard before. People rush all around to see who this guy with the mustache is. My pals are fillin' their pockets full of quarters.

Ike doesn't like all this attention see, so we head over to the blackjack tables. He sets hisself down and makes it pretty plain to even the dumbest ignoramus he don't want nobody else playin'. Everybody scatters when he reaches in his jacket and pulls out what looks like a hand-grenade, only it ain't, it's a cigarette lighter. He lights-up a big black Cuban cigar and blows smoke rings at the dealer. Then he says in very bad English, "Don't worry, infidel, it's just smoke, nothing nuclear, chemical or biological." Then he laughs a big belly laugh, pulls a big of pistol out of a shoulder holster and shoots a very large hole in the ceiling. Well, pretty soon the cops come and me'n Ike hustle out to the limo where Ali and the girls are waitin' with the motor runnin'. Seems Ike has had to leave places real fast before, places where there's lot's of sand and camels.

A little later that night we woke up an auto-dealer and Ike bought me a present, a big ol' red V-8 diesel truck. Brand-spankin' new it was, too. He just handed the dealer, who was still in his pajamas, a whole heap of greenbacks. Then he gave me a big hug and drove off in his limo. That's the last I saw of him. Wooee! I can't hardly wait to show it to the wife. She said I'd never amount to nothin'. Just look at me now. Yuh just never know when life's gonna hand yuh a little surprise.

That's all I can say about that night right now because of attorneys and certain government agencies and all. It's kinda hush-hush.

Ardes Shea

Ardes Shea was born in a small ranching community in central Utah. Following graduation from Millard County High School, she attended Utah State University. Her formal education was interrupted by WWII, and she spent the war years working in defense plants. She married James Shea, and they are parents to two children. She continued her education at Valley City Teacher's College, and taught school in North Dakota for three years. She has devoted most of her life to raising her family, gardening, and volunteer work. In her retirement years, she finds writing an interesting endeavor.

Hanford (A Continuation)

This is a continuation of an on going account of my experiences while assigned to a highly classified project during World War II.

Sometime during the night, I acquired a roommate: a very young, petite little gal who sobbed most of the night about having to say "goodbye" to her sailor boyfriend. I was too tired to be of much help in consoling her. She finally fell asleep about the time I arose to join the long line in the washroom.

Across from the administration building was the so-called executive mess hall. I had just enough time to get some breakfast before reporting for work. This mess hall was much like No. 8, but the people were much better dressed in business suits, dresses, heels and the like. The food was served in the same manner as the night before. After having some French toast and coffee, I found my way to the office where I had been assigned to work. I presented my papers to Mr. Hauser, the supervisor. I was then introduced to the rest of the office staff. Most were people much older than I. There were twelve desks in the office, lined up in two rows. In the rear of the office were several file cabinets. The first desk belonged to Mr. Hauser. Behind his desk was seated Mr. Pelke, assistant supervisor, then Mr. Holmes, an elderly gentleman. I never did find out what his position was. I was led to the next desk.

"This is where you will work," Mr. Hauser informed me. "This department receives copies of all orders for excess material. It is our responsibility to expedite these orders, and when the orders are received, we present the proof of receipt to the cost accounting department. Since your desk has the only phone with access to an outside line, your particular job will be to expedite by phone any orders that are marked CRITICAL. All orders, bills of lading, and receipts will come across your desk. You are to read them, initial them, and then put them in the basket on the desk behind you. But there is one thing that everyone does in this office: we look busy at all times, especially if someone comes into the office. You are to take a morning break before noon and another break in the afternoon. We address each other by our last names. I guess that covers everything, but if you have any questions, feel free to ask."

Mid afternoon, Mr. Hauser made an announcement to all office personnel. "I just received a call from Richland," he said, "and it seems that there is a bad dust storm headed our way. Close the windows, cover all machines, and leave for your barracks immediately." We all did as we were told. Outside, the air was a strange, eerie calm; but by the time I had been checked through the security gate, it had become very dark. I hurried along the sidewalk toward the barracks. Then the wind started to blow. The sand felt like pellets hitting my skin, and it became so dark it was difficult to see where I was going. Everyone was in a hurry and bumping into each other. It was then that I realized why the guards had said, "Keep to the right." It became dark as night, and then the thunder and lightning started, followed by a pounding downpour of rain. It wasn't just raining rain: it was raining mud. Not seeing where I was going, I stepped off the sidewalk and sank into gooey mud up to my ankles. Now I knew why the guards kept saying, "Stay on the sidewalk."

Exhausted, I finally made it to the gate of 25A. The guards at the gate let me take cover in the guardhouse until the rain let up a bit. I was soaking wet; my clothes were brown with mud and my hair was all matted with clumps of mud. I took off my shoes and made it the rest of the way to the barracks barefooted.

Entering my room, I thought, "I should have taken my umbrella along." But when I went to look for my umbrella in the closet, I discovered that it wasn't there. As a matter of fact, there wasn't anything in my closet. My clothes were all gone, and so was my roommate.

"Good lord," I thought, "what do I do now? Here I am, dripping wet and covered with mud, in the only clothes I own."

After washing my hair, which had now started to turn to globs of cement, I went in search of my footlocker.

"Someone got away with all of my clothes-and my umbrella," I complained to the guards at the gate.

"I wish we could be of more help to you," one of the guards said, "but this sort of thing happens all the time and there is not much we can do about it."

"Well, if you don't want me to embarrass this whole darn project by showing up for work tomorrow in these muddy clothes, you could tell me where the transportation building is, where I hope to find my footlocker."

"Well, I think I can do better than that," the guard said. "If you want to wait about five minutes until my relief arrives, I will drive you there in the squad car."

"That would be very nice," I agreed.

The weather by now had completely changed, looking very innocent, as if the violent storm had never occurred.

The guard offered to help locate my footlocker in the transportation building. This big warehouse was filled with piles of footlockers. Although it seemed impossible, we did manage to find a footlocker with my name on it.

As we drove back to the barracks, the guard said, "I would suggest that you keep your belongings locked in your footlocker, and push it as far back under your bed as you can. It's no guarantee, but it might help against robbery."

"Thank you for your advice and also your help," I said gratefully.

Returning to the barracks, I changed into some dry clothes and headed for the laundry room, which consisted of tubs, wash boards, and rows of clotheslines.

"I should tell you," the housemother said, "that it is not wise to leave any clothes unattended in the laundry room. You might want to dry your clothes in your own room."

I told her that my roommate had apparently left and so had all the clothes in my closet. "I'm sorry, "she said; "I should have warned you about leaving anything in your room that can just be picked up and carried off."

Some weeks later, I dropped in at what was billed as a rummage sale in the south end of the barracks. There, among other things, I found my clothes, for sale. Since these were people I did not want to confront, I just bought back a couple of my dresses. I felt badly that I had once thought that my roommate had taken my clothes.

"Hi, my name is Marion Page from Superior, Wisconsin, and I think you and I are the only two 'damn Yankees' in this office. Maybe we could go on break together."

"I would like that very much," I agreed. "How much time are we allowed for our break?" I asked as we left the office.

"As long as it takes," she said. "There is usually a long line to get into the rest room and an even longer line at the Coke station. The thing to do is to get a Coke near the back of the cooler; it will be frozen to a thick slush. That way it takes longer to drink it."

"How about Mr. Hauser? Doesn't he care how long we are gone on our breaks?"

"No, not really. When we are out of the office, he doesn't have to worry about us looking busy; we don't have to worry about trying to look busy; and he doesn't have to feel so guilty about he and his secretary spending the whole afternoon out of the office."

"Can I ask you something? How do you manage to look busy when there is nothing to do? I would never have believed how difficult it is to pretend to be busy."

"Oh, I just pretend to look for a file in one of those filing cabinets; and by the way, their filing system is a mess. The gal who sits at the desk next to mine files her fingernails so low they are almost bleeding, and then she can spend the whole next week watching them grow out."

"Well, Mr. Pelke just paces back and forth all day long, and poor old Mr. Holmes just sits and stares out the window. I try to write a letter to my folks every day but, since our mail is censored, there isn't much I can tell them except that I am fine and they are not to worry."

"I have been here two months now; it seems like an eternity. I worry about my dad. I am the only one he has, and he wasn't exactly thrilled with the idea of me taking off to places unknown. But as for everyone else, the war effort seems to be the only thing that is important these days."

Page and I became very good friends, and I really felt that I needed a friend. The other people in the office were older and married, with families back home in Oklahoma, Alabama, and

Mississippi. Their husbands also worked at this project but were housed in different barracks.

The barracks were not exactly a pleasant retreat after work. They were cold and bare, and strictly a place to sleep. There were no radios in the barracks; so here, too, as at work, except for doing my laundry, there was absolutely nothing to do. I did play a lot of solitaire. My only friend at the barracks was Chris, the housemother. She was most helpful to me, and we always managed to check on each other every night before we went to bed.

"The safest place in the barracks is in your room," she had said, "and since you cannot lock your door, try to push something against the door. If there is a commotion in the hall, don't go to investigate; just stay in your room and stay alert." The guards, whom I also found to be very helpful, had echoed this same warning.

Eating in the mess hall was never a pleasant experience. The food was nothing that appealed to me: grits, hominy, black-eyed peas was the usual fare served with catfish or chicken that was often referred to as "South American buzzard." I could manage to get through some green-looking French toast, greasy bacon, and coffee for breakfast. But for lunch, we were usually served whatever had not been eaten for supper the night before and called "fricassee of-whatever."

Not only was the food uninviting, the atmosphere was indeed hazardous. I cannot remember being in the mess hall when a fight did not break out. Dishes, food, pots, pans, and people would come soaring through the air. Like everyone else, I learned to dive under the table in a hurry.

Page and I decided to check out the one grocery store on the project in hopes of finding something we could eat, but found that most things there had to be cooked and we couldn't cook in our rooms. And one had to have ration stamps for most canned items. I thought maybe I could get a can of tomato soup and let the hot water run over the can to heat it, but that was a poor idea since the water was never any more than lukewarm. We finally settled for a few jars of baby food. This was something that was already prepared and didn't require ration stamps.

There was a theater on the project, and they were able to get the first run of the movies, but it just was not safe to be out after dark. However, Page and I did manage to take in matinees on Saturdays or Sundays. A dance was held every Saturday night and they were able to get the top bands. Here again, safety was the main consideration. A recreation hall was also available, but this was definitely not a safe place to be. In Washington, there was a law that anyone drinking beer had to be seated at a table and, since there were always more people than could be accommodated, the real wars were fought at the recreation hall.

I found the guards to be most helpful. "The most dangerous time around here is just before and just after payday. Everyone is broke before payday and everyone has cash after payday. When you aren't at work, it is a good idea to stay in your room," they had advised. On payday, we were given vouchers that then had to be cashed. Since there were no banks, there was the problem of what to do with the cash-a problem I had never faced before. I tried to send money home, but our mail was censored and somehow the money was always removed. Since it wasn't safe leaving money in my room or carried in my purse, I made myself a money belt and also strapped some in my shoe, something like an arch support.

As far as what the real purpose of this project was, no one seemed to know, ask, or even care any more. Just survival became the main and only priority.

I quite often offered to stay in the office and hold down the fort during the noon hour, since it beat going to the mess hall. On one such day, I received a call from top security inquiring about a specific order. I finally found the folder containing the information on the order. Page was right: this filing system was impossible; but I remembered her saying that most folders were put in the "miscellaneous" drawer, which was where I found this one. This order was marked critical and top priority. I had no idea what this order was for as it was named "fly eye."

Getting back to the telephone I said, "This order has been shipped and should reach the project today in Burlington car No. 887201. The destination is Area 21."

"Thank you so much."

The next call was from food services and they were not happy about an order for large coffee pots, which they felt should have been received a week ago. I again went in search of the folder containing the order. I explained to them that this order was LCL-less carload-and was held in Chicago until the car was full before it was sent on. I assured them that our office would follow up on the order.

I again received a call from top security. "In regard to the order for `fly eye' of which I spoke to you earlier, we have a bit of a problem which you just might be able to help us with. Past shipments of such materials have been tampered with. It is important that we find out whether such invasion of this material was made before or after it reached the project. It is important that we get this information without raising any suspicion. This might be easier accomplished by someone outside of our department, such as you."

"But I have no idea what this material is, or how to tell if it has been tampered with."

"You don't have to know anything except the name and number of the car in which it is being shipped, which you should memorize. Do not write this information down anywhere. All you have to do is see if the door on this car is sealed shut or if the seal has been broken. This is a highly restricted area, so your problem is getting into the area. We cannot grant you a pass without raising suspicions, so you will be entirely on your own. As important as it is to get this information, you have plenty of reasons to refuse. You have five minutes to think about it. There will be a car out in front of the administration building to take you to the area. If you decide to do this, leave the office now without telling anyone where you are going; but if you decide not to, we will understand."

"I don't know whether I want to do this or not," I thought to myself. "I could get fired for leaving the office without permission, or I could get arrested for trying to enter a restricted area. But oh, what the hell? It's going to be a long, boring afternoon around here, so I might just as well go for it."

I decided to leave my purse on my desk: the less I had with me, the better. I felt a bit naked not carrying anything, so I grabbed the folder with the order for coffee pots and walked out of the office. As I was promised, there was a squad car with two guards waiting in front of the administration building. We traveled over very dusty roads and passed several construction sites. I had no idea that this project covered so much area. Off to the right we passed what seemed to be a big city, a city made up of trailer houses. I didn't dare ask any questions; however, one guard did offer some information. "That trailer court houses forty thousand people," he said, "families of workers."

We passed another site where there were lots of men working. The one thing different about this site was that there was an Indian there, dressed in ceremonial garb. The guard explained, "They are moving the Indians' graveyard, and their chief is here to oversee it. This land was once an Indian reservation, and they agreed to have their village moved; but they still have exclusive rights to fish for salmon on the Columbia River."

We passed another unusual site: a large, round, deep hole in the ground that, I would guess, was about a half-mile in diameter. "They call this the salad bowl," I was told. I wanted to ask what they were stirring up down there, but I didn't.

We finally reached an area with all kinds of warning signs: "This is a restricted area," "absolutely no admittance to any unauthorized personnel." As we arrived at the gate, two well-armed guards met us.

"Do you have some authorization to be in this area?" I was asked.

"No, I don't. I work in receiving of excess material department, and I am trying to locate a car containing large coffee pots that might have been mistakenly sent to this area. I am really trying to get Food Service off my back." I showed him the folder. They went into conference. I sat there scared half to death. What an unbelievable excuse I had given for being there; they would never believe me. As they returned to the car, I really expected to be arrested.

"Come with us," one of the guards said as they led me up to the gate. "You will have to go through the detection chamber." Then they led me a short distance to where the train was just arriving. We watched as each car entered the station. The LCL car was not there; however, I did just happen to notice that the seal was broken on the door of Burlington car No. 887201. "Well, food service is going to be disappointed, but their shipment is not here. Thank you so much for allowing me to check." I again had to go through the detection chamber, and I was greatly relieved to be able to leave this area.

Arriving back to the administration building, I realized I had been away from the office all afternoon. How was I going to explain to Mr. Hauser? "Take the offensive," I told myself. With this in mind, I walked up to his desk still holding that dumb folder and said, "Mr. Hauser, our files really need some work done on them. I have had some experience in this area, and if you wouldn't mind, I would like to revise them and set up a cross-reference card file. It would make the office more efficient." I knew he didn't have the slightest idea of what I was talking about, but he readily agreed. "Here is a requisition form," he said. "Decide what you need and I will get it for you. If you need extra help, I'll get that, too."

"Thank you very much. If it is okay with you, maybe Page could help me on this."

"Sure thing."

Before I punched the time clock, I made a quick call to security. "The seal was broken," I said.

"Thank you; we really appreciate this," he said. "Oh, by the way, as a matter of curiosity, how did you manage to get into that restricted area?"

"No sweat. How much harm could be done by a pint-sized office clerk looking for a shipment of coffee pots?"

My Mother

One of my favorite pictures of my mother is just a simple snapshot. She is sitting on a stool out in her garden, wearing a straw hat, with her hoe in her hand. Gardening had always been a part of her life and something she really enjoyed doing.

There was a time, during the Depression, when raising a garden was necessary in order that there might be food for the family during the summer, and she always canned enough for an adequate winter supply. In the minds of most farmers, gardening is "woman's work," even though it is very hard work. My mother, however, didn't seem to mind the work so much; she really seemed to enjoy doing it.

"I just love to watch things grow," she used to say. "You just have to keep out the weeds, see that the plants get water, and keep the soil worked up around those tender plants so that they can grow."

Nearing her 90th birthday and now stooped, gray, and suffering from painful arthritis in her knees, she still insisted on raising a garden. Because it was too painful to stand and hoe, she would place a stool out in her garden and there she would sit, hoe in hand, making life miserable for any weeds within a five-foot radius. She would then move her stool to another site and keep right on working on those weeds. Sometimes a neighbor kid would come running over and offer to move her stool for her.

"I like to get out early, about the time the sun comes up," she would say, "and then again toward evening. I just can't seem to take the heat like I used to."

One of her prized possessions was her hoe. It, too, was old, and the blade had been worn to about half its original size.

"You need a new hoe, Grandma," everyone said.

"Oh, no, I don't," she would answer. "This is just the way I like it. The handle isn't so long or heavy and I've spent years getting that blade worn down the way I want it. It also serves as a cane to get me out to my garden and back."

"You sure have a beautiful garden," her neighbor commented when he stopped by. "You must have a green thumb."

"Oh, I don't think a green thumb has anything to do with it," she offered. "It's more important to have a dirty thumb. Anyone can have a garden, but it is important that you enjoy working in it. It's the best place in the world to solve your problems. God always seems to be there to listen to you."

"What are you going to do with all this produce?" people would ask.

"Oh, I give it to the kids and the neighbors. I can a lot of it and, anyway, it's just real good eating."

She used to rather enjoy watching from her window as little kids would crawl through her fence and fill their pockets full of peas. "I feel sorry for the kids today. The younger women don't raise gardens ever since that sewing factory started up in the old schoolhouse and all the women went there to work. Kids don't know what it is to pick fresh vegetables from a garden."

No Vacancy

Since we had missed going up north to see the leaves, we decided to catch their full beauty in the southern part of the state down around Red Wing. We started our little trip after school on a Friday afternoon. It was decided that we would drive until dark, find a motel, and spend all day Saturday enjoying the beauty of the season.

As it started to get dark, we began looking for a motel. I was surprised to see all the "no vacancy" signs. "I thought everyone went north to see the leaves, so why are all the motels full?" I asked.

"Oh, it's still early; we'll find something," Jim assured me; but now even the second-rate motels had "no vacancy" signs. When we stopped for gas, we were told that this was October Fest and everything had been booked far in advance. "There is an old hotel in Red Wing, not much, but you may be able to stay there," the attendant told us. "St. James Hotel, right on Main Street-you can't miss it."

Sure enough, there it was, right on Main Street: "St. James Hotel" in bold letters. The lobby was dark and rather spooky with only a small light bulb in the back over a desk. We cautiously made our way back to the desk. There was a little bell on the counter with a sign that said, "Ring for Service." No sooner had we rung the bell, than a small, half-stooped, beady-eyed character appeared at the window.

"Could we get a room?" Jim asked. He looked us over real carefully and then in a squeaky little voice said, "You just sign this register." With his hooked hand, he handed me a pen. "Good Lord," I thought, "this is like something out of the movies."

"That will be $9.00," he said, "$3.00 per person." After we had registered and paid our $9.00, he rang that little bell. Glancing over my shoulder, I saw this creature limping toward us. "Peter Lorre, as I live and breathe, the same squinty little eyes and sly, devious smile on his face," I thought.

He picked up our suitcases and, dragging one leg, led us to the elevator. "Step up," he said. There was a good six inches between the elevator and the floor. I am never comfortable in an elevator, and this one was the worst. He closed the cage-like door and pulled the lever to start the elevator. It jerked and clanged as it started to move. He pulled the lever again and the elevator jerked to a stop. "Step down," he said. We stumbled off the elevator and were led to room 204. This was a room out of another century: feather beds, one chair, and a sink that sat on a pedestal.

"What is that window above the door?" Pat asked.

"That's a transom," I said.

"What's its purpose?" she wanted to know.

"I'm not sure. I remember them in my grade school, and someone was assigned to open them in the morning and close them when school got out. I think it had something to do with the ventilation," I said.

"Do you mind if I close it?" she said; "I don't want someone or something crawling through there during the night."

The bathroom was across the hall. The bathtub sat up high on four legs. I only remember seeing one other bathtub like this in my life. Since Pat and I were both allergic to the feather beds, we sniffed and sneezed most of the night.

In the light of day, there seemed to be a great deal more charm about this place than I had imagined the night before. Since we had no desire to face that elevator or the bellhop, we decided to take the stairs down. It was a large, open stairway which led to the lobby, where hung a large, beautiful chandelier. Pictures of famous, important people who had stayed there lined the walls in the lobby. It was quite impressive.

Marjorie Stokes

I'm back again in our yearly publication. The statistics remain the same except that I reluctantly gave up the homestead for a retirement apartment. Less work but no more time—still 24/7. I'm gearing down. The chassis is showing wear. The passing gear is a thing of the past, and compound low is the order of the day. But the wheels are still turning. Memories are still sweet but relating them clearly and succinctly becomes more difficult. Spontaneity and enthusiasm seem lost in time. Still, we still put pen to paper (or fire up the computer) to share with readers the anecdotes and reflections of earlier times that are as out-of-date as the dinosaurs. Welcome!

Some Accoutrements on Memory Lane

I live with memories, as one is prone to do as the years roll by. Some of them are prompted by material things that have been passed down to me. Some I use in daily life; others were squirreled away in trunks and boxes. Many came to light when I downsized to a retirement apartment. They are precious, not monetarily perhaps, but rich in reminders of life in simpler times, now long gone by.

I think of my grandmother when I occasionally use the salad plates bordered in leafy brown vines. They belonged to her good set of dishes that I remember from the big farm house on Diamond Lake, and then the small "hired man's house" where they moved when Uncle Eddy married Elma Johnson. Uncle Harold and Aunt Agnes and their two daughters had occupied the small house until they had started farming on their own, a half mile west but still on the shores of Diamond Lake. And, in a gift box in a trunk, I found a fringed square of black taffeta whose folds have deteriorated to mere threads. My mother told me it was Grandma's confirmation head scarf from the Old Country, Sweden.

In the trunk, I also found the pince nez that my father wore occasionally, eye glasses held in place by a spring at the bridge of the nose. When I teased to try them on, they pinched my nose! In the same trunk, I found a leather coin purse shaped like a pouch with a clasp top, inscribed "Merchants and Farmers State Bank of Grove City." And I wondered what had become of the graceful oval snuff box engraved with his initials, SAL, for Swan Aron Liedholm on its cover. It had ended up in the junk drawer instead of an antique shop.

I wear my mother's wedding ring from 1910. Displayed on the roll top desk is the Tiffany vase that held beautiful gladioli from Pete Christianson's garden before I used it to hold the ones I raised just as successfully. Bachelor rural mail carrier Pete rented an upstairs bedroom from us during my childhood so seemed a part of the family. He helped my brother with algebra, and I raided his bookcase for Harold Bell Wright and Zane Grey novels, among others, as I grew up. While the Tiffany vase graced the dining room in season, my mother's favorite flowers, delicate perfumed sweet peas, found their place on the kitchen table in a footed graceful hand holding a cone-shaped vase. I wonder what happened to it after I left home. And I still use a few of my mother's linens, though they are frail and failing. Dresser scarves were needed in the many bedrooms, and they bloomed with flowers and were edged in delicate crocheted borders. Some of them are rolled in my linen drawer to this day, but I rarely use them for I doubt they would withstand washing and starching and ironing. On the shelf above the kitchen stove, I still use the cut glass salt and pepper shakers with their ornate sterling silver caps. They were displayed in the china closet among the cut glass stemware and Haviland china that I have since handed down to my daughter. An intriguing shapely china jar with a knobbed lid in that china closet always fascinated me for it was never used. Much later, I learned from an antique dealer that it was meant to hold oyster crackers. And a silver framework holding a mottled red glass jar had a tongs suspended from it, for sugar lumps, of course. More lowly is the toothpick holder I still use, picturing the stately brick Grove City school on its curved surface, a souvenir from about 1918, before my time.

I remember the cozy kitchen when I wind the clock that stood on the clock shelf now keeping time, with its swinging pendulum behind the gold design, on my buffet.

The intricate carved frame work is walnut. When my daughter had it repaired, the clock shop said it dated from about 1890, so I applaud it each Sunday when I wind it for keeping perfect time for over a century.

My older sister brought back from the Netherlands in 1938, the year Queen Elizabeth was crowned and before Hitler ravaged Europe, a picture entitled "The Yellow Lady" by Holbein, a print, of course. I thought it quite ugly at the time, but now I treasure it on my living room wall as a reminder of that long ago time. My sister Ruth loved pins, brooches as she called them, and I think of her when I wear them. And she did hardanger embroidery, so I carefully launder, starch and iron a dresser scarf from among her linens and think of the hours under her busy fingers.

My husband grew up in a big family in east Texas and left home for the big world early on, so he literally had nothing from his childhood until his sister gave him a china elephant that he remembered. The howdah on the elephant's back is an ash tray, and the panniers held matches and cigarettes, a treasure only because of its family connections. My son now has it.

What shall I do with a small girl's dress found in the trunk? It was my own, of course, before I even started school. I have no memory of wearing it, but my mother told me she saved it as it one of the few things she made for me herself. She hated sewing, and there were always dressmakers available. It is a red dress with small white polka dots, with the neck and front opening trimmed in a double line of lace, also adorning the short sleeves. I think of the washing and starching, and then the monumental task of ironing the lace so it stood in frills. In this changed world, I doubt my granddaughters would give it a second glance.

I have wallowed long enough in memory. In truth, I live in the present, a day at a time, but I feel life is enriched by the lives that have touched ours and made it good.

I Go Shopping In Litchfield

Big Crowd In Town *Nov. 13 1925*
There was an immense crowd of shoppers in town all day Thursday, the opening day of the final sale of the Greenberg stock of merchandise. The jam was so great at times that it was necessary to close the doors. The stock was greatly depleted during the day on which the weather was ideal. The grocery department was all but cleaned out. M.H. Greenberg, the late owner of the store, would have turned green with envy had he seen the crowd.

.....

The time of which I write happened before I started school. The Greenberg Department store went bankrupt in the fall of 1925, so my fifth birthday would be coming up in November.

Alice Floren, across the alley, asked my mother if she would like to go to the "going-out-of-business" sale. Mother was perhaps surprised, as she and Alice were not "bosom buddies," being too unlike in temperament. Alice was a driving ambitious woman with some pretensions even though she was the wife of a rather unsuccessful shoe store owner. (When his shoe store was sold years later, many of the boxes that lined his shelves were found to be empty.) Though Mother was the banker's wife, her dear friends on the block were Gertie Carlson, a widow raising two teen-age sons on her own, Beatrice Nelson, the cop's wife, and Mildred Peterson, whose husband was a trucker. The "coffee'd" together, involving much laughter and camaraderie.

Alice drove their square two-door Oldsmobile with aplomb and ventured far afield, considered quite daring in that day and age. My mother did not drive. On rare occasions we took the local train to Litchfield and Willmar when we shopped.

Still, it seemed a fortuitous chance, and my mother accepted. I was a clinging child, and where my mother went, I went. I was wildly excited by the prospect of "going to the sale." Our lives in Grove City in the 1920's were strictly slow lane. Church going, attending PTA meetings, visiting, "entertaining" people for meals about ran the gamut of our social lives.

So when we saw Alice open the garage door on its balky track, we were ready, watching from the kitchen window. I folded down the front seat and climbed in the back, and the ladies occupied the front seat.

And off we went to Litchfield, nine miles away!

Fortunately, I was an observant child. We cruised down Sibley Avenue, but there was not a parking place to be had near the store. Evidently many others were attending the Big Sale.

We circled several blocks and finally found a diagonal parking spot beside the community park (where the city band gave concerts each Saturday night in the octagonal bandstand during the summer), almost three blocks from the store and headed back toward Grove City to boot, but at least we were on the same side of the street as the store.

I tagged along behind the ladies, peeping into the store windows. Scarp's Cafe especially fascinated me. Sometimes when we took the morning local to Litchfield, we would eat at Scarp's before we came home on the afternoon train. It was a long narrow room with lazily-moving ceiling fans and enclosed wooden booths with lattice work at the top lining the side of the room opposite the counter. I always thought of a gypsy wagon, though I had certainly never been in one.

Today, shopping was our purpose. The interior of the Greenberg store had embossed tin ceilings and closely-ranked counters and display shelves. The fascinating part to me was that, when a purchase was made on the main floor, the clerk put the money in a wooden cup, put the sales receipt in a clip on the bottom, pulled a wooden handle sharply, and the cup flew on cables-to the open balcony, where a cashier made change and sent the duplicate sales slip and change back down the wire in the cup to the correct counter.

Today, the aisles were mobbed. One could hardly move in the press of shoppers. Mother and Alice inched their way along. At first, I kept a hand on Mother's skirt, but soon I was distracted by the displays and the crowds of shoppers.

Suddenly, I found myself in a crowd of strangers. I was too short to see above the press of grownups, and I was much too timid to call out. I groped my way among the ladies' skirts but could find no familiar one.

I was lost! My insides shrunk as I realized my predicament. I was a sheltered child with no experience in unexpected situations. But I don't remember any panic, though a sinking feeling seized me. Taking stock, I first decided to thread my way back to the entrance and just wait until my mother and Alice came out. But there was another street-front entrance and a side door, too, that came out of the shoe department. So that was not a sure course of action.

Still I lingered a while (perhaps a very short while) inside and then outside the door. Neither Mother nor Alice appeared. Searching the store to find my mother would be like looking for a needle in a haystack.

These many years later, I am still amazed at my presence of mind, as sheltered and pampered as I had always been. I decided that they would have to return to the car in due time, and I was quite sure that I could find my way to it. I had two cross streets to cross, and I "stopped, looked and listened" at each one. I was reassured to pass Scarp's and I remembered a corner drug store, and the Penney store was at the last corner where the park began.

Now I felt more confident for I knew I would recognize Alice's car-it stood often in the gravel parking strip in front of their garage. Mid-block I found my sanctuary. Car doors were not locked in those days, and I was soon in the back seat, safe and secure. And Alice had left the cream-colored gloves she was never without, on the front seat. No doubts now.

I don't know how long I sat there. But suddenly the door opened and there was my mother! I hadn't shed a tear during my perilous journey back to the car nor during my long numb wait, but when I saw Mother, I burst into a loud wail of pure relief and clung to her.

"There, there," she comforted.

When I had calmed down, she asked, "Do you want to come back with me to the store? I'll have to find Alice. She is still looking for you. I decided I'd take a long chance and see if by any means you had found your way back to the car."

I opted to stay in the car. I knew they would be returning, and I was through adventuring for one day-I didn't want to chance getting lost again.

That evening, at the supper table, my mother was recounting the day's events to my father. I was only partially aware of their conversation being lulled toward sleepiness by the excitement of the day.

"I was beside myself," my mother said. "Alice and I searched everywhere and asked clerks and even perfect strangers if they had seen a little girl in a green plaid cape and fuzzy tam. As a last resort, I left Alice in the store in case Marjorie should turn up, and I went back to the car. I could see that fuzzy tam in the back window before I reached the car. You can't believe the relief I felt."

My father looked at me kindly. "She'll get along all right. She can use her head. I'm proud of her."

My busy father, involved in bank and community affairs, was somewhat a stranger to me. Those words of approval warmed me through and through.

"I am positively amazed at her presence of mind," my mother said. "I feel we have sheltered her almost too much."

"But she has smarts," my father said.

I sleepily let the accolade register in my mind. But, for now, I was ready for bed. Not only had I had a hair-raising experience, but I had missed my nap.

Winter Washday

When I was a very young child, washday provided some drama in an otherwise prosaic, life-a day that transformed the tidy orderly kitchen into an arena of action that was intriguing.

Good Lutheran that my mother was, she defied her Maker in her need to organize her work week. On Sunday evening, the copper washboiler was placed on the Monarch kitchen range and filled with soft rainwater from the middle faucet on the sink which had access to the cistern under the back porch. My mother shaved gold-orange Fels Naptha soap into a saucepan, added water, and set it on the stove to soften before she added it to the boiler.

Next, the Speed Queen washing machine must be retrieved from its home on the screened back porch where an old oilcloth tablecloth protected it, though the thick gnarled grapevine on the north side of the porch at least strained the wind and snow. It was a zinc-colored square tub with a rounded bottom to accommodate the mesh metal cylinder which held the clothes as it revolved in the soapy water. A latched door on the cylinder permitted clothes to be put in and taken out. A platform low on the legs held the bulky electric motor, and a swivel wringer was firmly attached to the top. We wrestled the squeaky-wheeled monster into the middle of the not-very-large kitchen, crowding the drop leaf table into the corner by the radiator.

Then, a folding slatted rack was positioned back of the washer, and on it were placed the two rinse tubs, the last one being liberally "blued" by a dollop from the bottle of Mrs. Stewart's blueing, which supposedly made the clothes look whiter. These tubs were filled, also with cistern water, on Sunday night so they would warm up somewhat overnight.

Islands of sorted clothes ringed the edge of the kitchen. Narrow aisles allowed us to get to the range, the sink, the basement door, the bathroom door, the dining room door, and the door to the backstairs and to the back porch. My mother often complained about a kitchen that had seven doors and two windows with minimum wall space. Even so, she had a plushy love seat with carved wooden edging taking up space, for the kitchen was an all-purpose room that needed seating. It was often my perch when I watched the goings-on in the kitchen to keep out of the way.

When the white clothes that needed soaking and boiling had been put into the soapy water of the copper boiler and covered, we could retire for the night. It was a short night for my mother, as she rose at four a.m. to get the show on the road.

I liked to wake to the throbbing sound of the washing machine, knowing my mother was already beginning her long day. In my cozy bed, I assume I must promptly have fallen asleep again for I had a recurring dream that seemed so real to me that I secretly believed it to be so. Streams of rabbits trooped through the north window, across the bedroom, and out the door to the dining room. They must have been dressed for school as they looked like the Peter and Mopsy and Cottontail rabbits in my story book. I was wise enough never to mention them to anyone (until now) because I was sure they would have been met with disbelief.

But I tried to be up as early as I could make it out of bed so I could slip through the swinging door, in pajamas and slippers, and roost on the love seat in the hot steamy kitchen, lit only by the single bulb that hung on its string from the middle of the kitchen ceiling.

"You up already?"

My mother would spot me no matter how quiet I was. She wasn't really cross, more like resigned.

"It's way too early. Do you want something to eat?"

"Oh, no. I'm not hungry. But I want to help. May I swish the clothes in the rinse tubs?"

"I suppose so, but stay away from the wringer, and try not to get wet."

I was in glory. Keeping dry was impossible, of course, even though I rolled up the sleeves of my pajamas. I loved to slop in water! I could use the plunger that resembled a tin funnel with a stick coming out the top. I could guide the folded clothes into the rinse on my side of the wringer and swoop them through the water. When Mother swung the wringer to the position between the tubs, I led the clothes into the bluing tub, opening them so the bluing would reach every fold. When she pivoted the wringer to the basket position, I shook out the clothes and led them into the oval woven reed basket.

But I must stay away from the starch until she was through using it. She had boiled lumps of white starch in a large kettle until it was gelatinous, then had thinned it with boiling water from the teakettle. She scrunched up shirts so only the collar, cuffs, and buttonhole strip were dipped into the starch. She starched aprons and blouse and petticoats. She had complaints from my brother and me. I remember bringing a petticoat to the kitchen and standing it upright to prove that it could stand by itself No matter. She starched.

Her washing had a pattern. The bulky white sheets and embroidered pillow case. made the first load. Next, the white clothes from the boiler that she retrieved with a stick, bleached from many washdays, into her big silver dishpan that had handles on each side, were dumped into the washer. Then, in order, came the colored clothes, the work clothes, then perhaps a rag rug to make use of the soapy water.

The clothes were washed, rinsed, and wrung, but that was not the end. All of the water must be emptied by pails into the kitchen sink. Then the tubs and boiler and Speed Queen must be wiped down before they were put back on the porch. Then the kitchen floor was wiped up. Only when the kitchen was orderly again did she give her attention to the baskets of wet clothes.

In the winter, she hung out only the sheets and pillow cases to freeze-she thought freezing whitened them. The clothesline was strung from the back porch to one Whitney apple tree, then to another, and then to the corner of the garage. Because of the distance between, she had thin pieces of lumber, with two nails driven into the top, that she kept in the garage. After she had hung the clothes, she inserted the clothesline between the nails midway between the fastened points and hoisted up the line, securing the other end on the ground or in a snowbank. The clothes were well above any possibility of sweeping the ground. She had bundled up well, but when she came in, she blew on her fingers and held them over the range.

"Weather not fit for man or beast," she'd remark, and then probably pour herself a cup of egg coffee from the pot that stood on the back of the range. I'm sure she had looked around the neighborhood for evidence of other clothes on lines. She liked to be first.

By then, my father was off to the bank and my brother off to school after skimpy breakfasts. Now the heavy baskets of wet clothes would be toted to the attic--up the backstairs, up the attic stairs to the spacious attic where lines were secured around nails driven into the rafters. She was, fortunately, a strong healthy woman whose farm background put her in good stead. It was cold up there-we put on sweaters-but it was a sheltered chill. Double windows in eaves on three sides permitted a rather dim light, and along the slanting walls were treasures, discarded though they were.

Now I was in heaven! There was so much to do and see. Even though I had been up there often enough, I was not allowed to play by myself when I was young. The spindly curtain stretchers had sharp pointy nails-I could pretend to be hanging my wash from among the odds and ends in the attic. I opened trunks and chests and looked, but I was not allowed to "dig". Old-fashioned clothes hung on nails. Old toys, old plush photo albums, old dishes, odds and ends of furniture, whatever, were in good order. I asked a million questions which my patient mother couldn't always answer for she had inherited this attic as a second wife. I wonder that she didn't throw things out, as she liked apple-pie order. But she was thrifty and in those Depression years, she found many thing of use in the attic that helped her "make do." She could retrim last year's Easter hat into a thing of new beauty and taste from what she scrounged in the attic.

Too soon for me she said, "Well, that's done. They may have to hang for a couple of days to dry."

Gathering up baskets and her almost empty clothes-pin apron, we headed down to the warm kitchen, duty done. However, the clean clothes needed more attention, in time. 'Taken down, many sprinkled, most of them ironed, all put away-part of the housewife's workweek. And those, some say, were the "Good Old Days."

I've had a lifetime of washing and ironing, and I still like it, I think, because of my warm childhood memories of that momentous day of the week. Our modern washers and dryers are so convenient that washday is not the ordeal it once was-nor as much fun to be involved in for today's children.

Carole Wendt

Carole Wendt was born on a farm south of Litchfield, Minnesota. She graduated from Litchfield High School, the University of Minnesota, and New York University. Her writing has appeared in magazines and newspapers, including the Litchfield Independent Review. She has produced and written for WNBC-TV News as well as such programs as the Today Show, the David Frost Show, and the Jack Paar Show. She now divides her time between Litchfield and her home in Manhattan's Greenwich Village. She is a member of the Litchfield Writers' Group.

Grandma's Thigh

I visited Grandma in the nursing home.

That's the Grandma of the silver hair and the toothless grin and the small round body. That Grandma.

As the nurse changed the bedding, I caught a glimpse of Grandma's thigh.

To my surprise, it was white, soft, unwrinkled. Actually, quite shapely.

Suddenly, because of that shapely thigh, I could see the young girl my grandfather had loved and desired.

Grandma died, they said, in her nursing home bed as she watched an early winter snowfall. The kind where the snowflakes are large and drift slowly to earth.

My brother said she always loved watching snow fall. He said, (he's very romantic), that her spirit had walked out into the snowflakes and met Grandpa who had been waiting for her for thirty-four years.

I think my brother's right.
I saw Grandma's thigh.

The Ghost Buildings of Litchfield

My brother, Calvin Peterson, and I were going to meet in Litchfield at the Office Supply store the other day. "Where is that place anyway? " he asked me. "It's across the street from where the Unique Theater used to be," I said, "and north of where the hotel was." After I said that, it hit me. I'm using ghost buildings to give directions. My brother grew up here, so he knew exactly where to look for the store.

When I drive around town, I see quite a few ghost buildings. Like the old courthouse. In my imagination it still sits on the corner facing Central Park. Tall, dark, imposing. It had a dignity the new one just doesn't have. I was too young to do business at the old building, but I liked the way it looked. It looked so important; a place where serious things happened. The new courthouse is low, angular, and rather informal. It does its job very well, but it's a little confusing in its layout. Am I right or when you come in on the main floor aren't you actually on the third floor? Something's funny about the setup. Those counters are all angles and seem to be arranged like little conversation nooks. Maybe the architect wanted to take away some of the awe inspiring aspects of the old fashioned castle-like courthouses.

I remember ice skating at a rink kitty-corner from the old high school building, which is now the Social Services Building. The skating rink is now a parking lot. I can't possibly forget the rink. I carry a scar on my left knee where I hit the curb running from the rink to the school. The rink was also the scene of my first date when I agreed to meet a young boy there for an afternoon of skating. I skated at that rink a lot, especially over

Christmas vacation. Many times, at the end of the day, exhausted, I walked to my grandmother's house three blocks away and took a nap, after a glass of milk and a sandwich.

I can still see the depot across the street from the old hotel. I remember standing by it years ago as a passenger train pulled in and Myrna, my eight-year-old sister, got off after a visit to her great aunt Katie Coyle. Myrna had ridden the train to and from Minneapolis all by herself. She was so thrilled she could do it. She came running toward us, all smiles, and my mother grabbed her and hugged her as if she'd been gone much longer than a week.

The hotel, demolished almost 20 years ago, was a central part of Main Street when I was growing up in Litchfield. It had a class of its own. Traveling salesmen stayed there and ate in its fancy restaurant. Fancy to me, anyway. The bus stopped there, too, and passengers waited in the coffee shop. My mother waitressed in the restaurant back in the Twenties and often talked about the interesting people who passed through town. Once when I was a child, she arranged a meeting with a man who was staying at the hotel. He offered lessons in playing the Hawaiian guitar. I tried to play, but I was left-handed and his guitar was strung for a right-handed player.

We used to watch movies at the Unique theater; it stood where a vacant lot now sits like a missing tooth on Main Street. I remember it was the custom to stand for the national anthem before the screening of the film or "show" as we called it then. I suppose that ended when the Second World War ended. I loved the Three Stooges, Gene Autry, and Roy Rogers. Many times my mother carried my little sister out of the theater. Movies put her to sleep like a charm.

West of Main Street sits a large open space where the Litchfield Produce used to be, the scene of many memories for me. I got my first job there, and I joined the union, too. At 16 I was a member of the Amalgamated Meat Cutters and Butcher

Workmen; affiliated with the AFL/CIO. I attended union meetings and as a teenager I learned the importance of organizing and sticking up for your rights and of not being afraid of your boss. I also learned how to make time pass without boredom even while breaking eggs for eight hours interrupted only by bathroom breaks (five minutes, girls!) and a half hour for lunch. Most of us ate lunch at Kate Pierce's little restaurant nearby. She served heavenly hot beef sandwiches; they weren't called "commercials" then. A tender roast beef sandwich alongside fresh mashed potatoes with a delicious gravy over all; fifty cents. It would have been great even if we hadn't been starving for four hours.

A town is like that, I guess. Layers and layers of ghost buildings, one over the other depending on how old the eyes are that look at them. I guess every generation has its own private village. They see different ghost buildings as time passes. Every so often, though, a building here or there stands for generations and we all see the same one. For a while. Until new ideas, fashion, whim, or reluctant practicality dictates that it, too, join the ghosts.

Buster and the Barbed Wire

For the first eight years of my life, I lived on farms. Mostly, it was an idyllic life. But one bright sunshiny summer afternoon, a horse made a lasting and frightening impression on me. It happened on a farm north of Grove City. I was six years old and that day I was walking in the barnyard watching my father fill up the manure spreader inside the barn. He stood behind the wagon which was hitched to Buster, our stallion. Buster tossed his head; he didn't like being harnessed and he didn't like being in the dark crowded barn. He was irritated; I could tell that.

Buster always frightened me. My dad had a hard time controlling him. Then, as I stared at him about twenty feet away, he suddenly reared up and lunged forward, straining against the harness. I panicked and ran toward the house. Mother was there and I knew I'd be safe. Before I could get to the house, I slammed hard into the barbed wire fence. Two lines of barbs hit my right cheek. I don't remember pain but the shock of it wrenched screams and sobs out of me. I crawled under the wires and raced to the house, blood streaming down my face. Mother rushed to the door. She calmly cleaned off the blood and soothed me and put me to bed to calm down and rest. Stitches weren't necessary. No doctor looked at me; in those post-Depression days you didn't call the doctor for such a small accident. I healed up just fine and went on being a little kid.

In the right light you can see the faint scar lines I still wear from the barbed wires. But there's something else I've kept from that day on the farm. A fear of horses. I only rode once since then. Not with pleasure but to be part of the gang one day at a ranch. I'm very reasonable about it. I tell people horses are easily frightened and can jump sideways and dump a rider in a second. They are huge and when they step on your foot, you notice it. Not like when a cat steps on you. Or if they want to take a good look at you, they like to stare and slowly walk toward you without blinking. I tend to back up and leave the area.

That's what I did when I was a teenager and a boy I was dating came out to see me on his horse. He sat high up on his mount, cowboy hat and all, and chatted with me. I didn't pay much attention to him because his horse couldn't stop looking into my eyes. Then I noticed he was inching closer and closer to me. My boy friend didn't notice. He asked me if I'd like to ride with him. Well, no, I said, I have to go inside now and make some phone calls..or wash my hair.. or .. do dishes .. or lie down and die ..anything to get away from that pushy horse. I never rode his horse and I won't ride another one any time soon. I've got all those logical reasons about horses being dangerous and, all but now you know it's all about Buster and the barbed wire.

The Promise

Once upon a time, an old lady sat in her room in a nursing home. It was the end of a long day and she was lonely. She didn't get many visitors. Her children were busy or far away and most of her friends had died.

Then, the phone rang. It was a friend, a man she knew and liked very much and hadn't heard from for a long time.

He wanted to know how she was and then offered to bring her a favorite dish: clam chowder. He said, "For sure, day after tomorrow at one o'clock, I will come with clam chowder for you. Would you like that?"

The old lady was thrilled. "Oh, yes, I would like that very much!" A visit from someone she wanted to see ..and with a delicious dish she liked a lot. How wonderful. How wonderful.

That night, she went to bed thinking about the day to come and smiled to herself as she settled in for the night. That day, for a change, would be interesting. Something new: a visitor she hadn't seen for such a long time and a treat to eat, besides.

On the morning of the big day, the aides brushed and braided her hair carefully and she was happy. They helped her put on a special nice dress. She ate her breakfast and enjoyed it. Then, she came back to her room to wait. She was delighted to be waiting for something nice to happen. Noon came: her dinnertime. She told the girl who came to wheel her chair to the dining room that she had a visitor coming with a big bowl of delicious clam chowder.

She said, "I'll skip dinner so I'll have room for the clam chowder." Then, she waited. She sat in her wheelchair in her room, alone. But not sad, not lonely today. She was going to have a special visitor. A special treat. Time passed slowly. She waited longer and longer. Because she was blind, she couldn't see a clock but she knew too much time was passing. She was getting hungrier and hungrier and then ...sadder and sadder... as she realized the promise was not going to be kept. No one was going to come after all. There would be no clam chowder; no special visitor. She began to cry.

She sat in her wheelchair with her head down ..and the tears came for a long time. And then, it was time for supper. She no longer cared what the meal would be. She wasn't hungry anymore.

Holds On Happiness

I was reading a Jane Austen novel when I came across a passage in which one of the characters talks about holds on happiness. She is telling a friend about another friend who has discovered a passionate interest in daffodils. That is so wonderful, she says, now she has another hold on happiness.

A "hold on happiness." The idea started me thinking about what my "holds" were. I remembered the day. I told my brother, Calvin Peterson, about one of them.

We were driving around Minneapolis doing errands and decided to stop for a snack. I saw a bagel store and asked him if he'd ever had a bagel. "Yes," he said, "once." "What was it like?" I asked. "It had blueberries in it." "Oh, oh. That's not a bagel," I told him. "I'm from New York City and I know what a bagel is supposed to be like. Come with me. I'll order an authentic bagel in this place." I told the waiter to slice a plain bagel in half, smear it with cream cheese, add a slice of tomato, and a slice of onion, and then top it off with a slice of smoked salmon. Slam it all together; cut it in half and hand it over. He did.

"Now," I said, "that is a bagel the way it's supposed to be served. See what you think."

We silently chewed our way through the thing. When we finished, I asked, "So, what do you think?"

"That is really, really good. I like it."

"Well, now, you have another hold on happiness. Next time you're feeling blue, order that. It's dependable."

My other holds on happiness seem to be very simple ...and cheap, too. I get a mellow feeling of happiness just slicing through the water when I take a swim at the local motel pool. And I really get a kick out of floating in Lake Manuela staring up at fleecy white clouds drifting across a bright blue sky.

Then there's the mornings: I love to lie on my daybed, a cup of good coffee in hand, and watch the world pass by my porch windows. The caffeine lifts my spirits and the birds, squirrels and humans going about their business keep me in a gentle state of bliss.

I also get a good feeling when the lights go down at the movie house. I hunker down in my seat and smile as I wait for the film to start. An adventure is about to begin.

I like watching my sister, Myrna Maher, tell jokes. She gets a twinkle in her eyes and her whole body seems to rise up in anticipation as she captures the audience and leads them through her story. Then, the punch line; the listeners erupt into laughter. She smiles and her eyes half close in the pleasure she feels in making us laugh. I laugh at the joke but more than that, it makes me happy to see her so happy. Once again, she has woven a spell, taken us on an imaginary trip, and then, made us all laugh with her.

It's a pleasure watching people do what they're good at. I had my roof shingled a couple of years ago. I hired a man reputed to be very good at that. It turned out he was.

Even though I knew nothing about the roofing process, I could tell he was a professional. He worked efficiently, every night cleaning up debris left over from the day's work. He was confident without being arrogant. When he met my nephew, an expert in construction, who came by to take a look, he was unperturbed and welcomed him as a fellow professional. It was a pleasure to watch him move about the roof making steady and sure progress. Though I'm sure he knew I didn't know anything about roofing, he regularly reported on his progress and what he planned to do next. He started on time and finished when he said he would. He was expertise in action and as such, a pleasure to watch in action.

For me, driving is another reliable hold on happiness. A sunny day in the country, Strauss waltzes on the tape recorder, a good car, and me cruising the gravel roads passing by cornfields and cows, scanning the sloughs for ducks, herons, muskrats, turtles, maybe even a couple pheasants and a deer or two.

Sometimes people ask me how I can enjoy Litchfield after living in "big, exciting" New York City. I, on the other hand, wonder how they can ask me that. Don't they know what they have here?

Margaret Werner

This Fourth of July, Margaret was watching the Fourth of July program from Washington, D.C. When the Capitol and other D.C. sights were shown, "I became homesick. I almost wanted to go back there and live. There is so much to see and all of the art galleries and museums are free. I always watched the fireworks while parked on South Capitol Street which was only two blocks from my home. Homesick or not, I decided to stay in Minnesota--even with the mosquitoes!"

Bronchial Tubes

Do we need them?
Yes, we do.
Then why do mine
Not let the air go through?
I try so hard,
Breathe deep, they say.
But that just doesn't work,
Air can't get through.
I guess I forgot
To pull the cork out,
Letting the air, in,
Going to the lungs.
So to the doctor I go,
And he checks me out. "It's noisy in there,"
Says he as I breathe.
"Here's a prescription-
It should clear things up.
Making your bronchial tubes
Happy as happy as they can be."

The Indians I Saw and Met

The first time that I ever saw Indians was in Rapid City, SD. It was in the early1940's. I was working in the Woolworth's Dime Store at the toy counter. I ordered the items and was in charge of my counter.

I think that it was July or August when these two Indian ladies came in each carrying a baby wrapped in a blanket the size for a single bed. It was dark in color and the babies were asleep and didn't look to be too warm. They were pretty babies with round faces. The mothers were stout, good-looking ladies. They carried them as if there were nothing in their arms. I don't know what they bought because they never came to the toy counter.

Another day I was walking downtown and I saw a sight that I will never see again. A pickup truck was parked and an Indian lady was sitting in the bed of the truck. She looked so contented that I supposed that was where she enjoyed sitting. A man and a boy of about 10 got in the cab of the truck and away they went. I wondered how the baby ever got into the bed. I don't think that I could have.

My sister and I went for a walk every Sunday. This time we went west and walked a long ways and then stopped dead in our tracks. Up the street was a large wigwam, an older car parked in the yard, and in the crotch of the tree was a skeleton head of a deer. The Indian family lived there all year.

The next time I was going to beauty school in Yakima, WA. It was in September and there was a canvas fastened to the back of a brick building, forming a tent. There were a lot of them. You could see them from the alley. The brick building formed one side and the canvas the other side of the tent. This was not a very large space for someone to live in. When I first saw them, I couldn't imagine what they were for. I didn't have long to wait. I soon had an Indian lady who wanted a permanent. She was dressed nicely in a clean, pressed dress. She and all the other Indian ladies who I had as customers got our best permanents. The lotion used was thick and creamy. I think that the hair was conditioned as it permed. The price was $10.00.

The ladies were always nice, always quiet. Then one day I had a young Indian lady who was quite talkative. She was about 20 years old and they came from Canada to work in the hop fields. She had never been to school and I thought how sad this was. She could have been a secretary, teacher, clerk, or any position she wanted and any employer would have been happy to have her. She was such an attractive lady, but with no education, it would be more difficult for her. What a pity!

I became a beautician. I passed the state boards with the highest score of the two schools in Yakima. My field of work has been an enjoyable one.

While I was in Yakima, I went to an Indian religious celebration. We people could go on a Sunday evening, after their celebration was over. It lasted two days. We were lucky to find a place to park. Walking up to the tent, we saw three men playing a game with bones. Some women were playing also. There were several of these tables. There were children running around the big tent, laughing and having fun. We entered the tent and sat on the ground. The Indians were doing the same thing. There were three men at the opposite side of the tent playing drums, one larger than the other two. Sometimes they chanted as they played. There was a dance for the men and one for the ladies. During each dance, the men or the ladies formed a circle and had a dance step they did in a single file. All had sober faces as they danced.

No mother went out looking for her child. The child came in and sat down by the mother. Everyone was quiet--the only sound was the drums and chanting. It was very enjoyable. It was beautiful experience.

I never thought that I would see Indians in Washington, DC, but I did. I had an Indian stewardess but I don't know what airline she flew with. She came in to get her hair fixed and I did not ask her what tribe she was from. She had a light complexion. She said if she had children she would not bring them up in the Indian way. To teach the children not to cry, they would put their finger on the stove for a second. If the child cried, it would be repeated until the child could take the pain without crying. This was an important thing to learn. She also carried a gun, putting it under her pillow so if anyone got into her room, she could protect herself. Someone tried to do this once, but didn't get in.

I never imagined DC to have Indians at the Mall over the Fourth of July, but one year they did. The Indians were from Alaska. They were good-looking people with round, smiling faces who laughed and talked a lot. This was something that, to my knowledge, the Canadian Indians did not do.

The men were sitting on the ground on one end of their space and their children were laughing and playing around them. Some of the children were sitting on their laps. The ladies told us how they dried meat and stored it in a building to keep. If left outside, the wolves and bears would eat it. These people had the strongest teeth. They were the same size and length--no crooked teeth. Their smiles were so beautiful. I could hardly take my eyes off of their beautiful smiles showing their perfect teeth, so strong.

There was also a lady from Yakima, WA who was the person called if any Indian children were missing from school. She carried clothes with her as that was the reason some children were missing school. They had no clothes. She was a small, petite Indian lady. I wondered if she had mixed white and Indian blood. I had never seen an Indian who was so small.

There was also an Eskimo lady. She was very petite and very interesting to listen to. She told us how they made their snowshoes. Also, when she was a child, she played with the puppies but when they grew up and were hitched to the dog sleds, they were no longer a dog to be played with. It was all business from then on.

One time it was her turn to get the drinking water. It was two miles away. She hitched up the dogs to the sled and set out to get the water. Everything went well and she filled her cans and was about to start for home when a blinding snowstorm started. She couldn't see very far as she was blinded by the storm. She tried to get the dogs to move but they wouldn't budge. After several tries with no success, she let them go on their own. They took her home. If they had obeyed her, they would have been lost and may have frozen to death.

This was the best time I ever spent at the Mall. It all happened because there wasn't a big crowd.

Voting

I can't remember where I was working the first time elections came up in which I could vote. I know that I wasn't anxious to vote. I thought, "I don't know enough about these people." One never does. You hear the criticism of how bad each person is but do you hear of the things they would like to do if given the chance? Anyway, I did vote that year.

In the forties, I was working in Goldendale, WA in a beauty salon. It was located behind the barbershop. The walls were thick enough that sound couldn't be heard from one place to another. I think that Truman and Dewey were running and the town was pretty much Republican. The rumor spread around town that Dewey was a Catholic. The message was: "Don't vote for Dewey because if he wins, the Pope will be running the country." Now how the Pope would have time to do this, the paper never said.

I remember the day before the elections, the barbershop was full of men. Their talking was quite loud most of the time. I couldn't hear what they said, just the loud noise. I thought that they were Republican and were excited after the elections, maybe thinking of pushing Truman out. At the end of the day, I closed the shop, went to vote and thought tomorrow should be another noisy day in the barbershop. I could hardly wait.

All through the night, you couldn't guess who would win. They were that close. I went to bed not knowing who the winner was. It was an exciting time.

The next morning I turned on the radio to hear who had won. It was Truman! Oh, what will go on in the barbershop today, I thought. I was excited. When I got to work and walked past the barbershop, it was closed. "Why is that?" I wondered. Maybe he will open later. Well, he didn't open at all that day. No sounds came from the place. Was I ever disappointed! So ended that day.

The next interesting experience was when I worked in Washington, DC. I don't remember the year, I think that it was in the fifties, when elections came up the first time I was living there. I asked someone who they thought they would vote for. People in DC couldn't vote. Those who come in from other states can vote by absentee ballot, but those born here can't. Your absentee ballot has to be from your state. "That doesn't seem fair," I thought. That year I did vote by absentee ballot but never again. After all, I was now a Washingtonian. Really, it was sort of fun watching everyone else struggle as to who was the best man to vote for.

I always enjoyed the inaugural parades no matter who won. When Eisenhower won, the parade started at one o'clock and wasn't over until after five o'clock. It was the longest of all the parades while I was living there. Minnesota never had a float or a car in any of the parades, not even when Humphrey was

Vice-President. I was really disappointed. I called our state stingy. Florida and California always had floats.

I forget the year Congress decided to make some laws to let black people vote. Many states in the South did not allow black people to vote. The law was passed and people were very happy. By then there were a lot of black people living in DC. The word went out--black people in DC couldn't vote--no one could. Congress decided that they had to do something about it. The District of Columbia is a district, not a state, so new laws were passed and everyone could vote except foreigners.

The Sunday before the election there was a picture and statement about the men who were running in the paper. It was exciting. We could all vote for the president. The DC officials were still appointed by Congress. I think that by the next election, we could vote for a representative in Congress. However, he didn't have a vote. To me, that was nothing. He could try to get people to be on his side, but didn't have a vote.

It took several years before the DC people got to vote for mayor, city officials, and such. Before that, someone in Congress was appointed to place school board members and all city officials in office. This caused some problems. I had left DC in 1981 before the law was passed.

Life goes on, and this year I could again vote in Minnesota. I'm an independent so I'm not too unhappy about the person who wins. I feel that they will do the best job they can.

Jack Weyrens

Jack Weyrens presently serves as a part-time judge in Sibley County. He retired from full-time work in 2000 after twenty-eight years as a judge. He enjoys reading, driving and tinkering with old cars, working with wood, and spending time.

Main Street

Those who know me well will tell you that one of my favorite pastimes is to sit and dream of days gone by. Perhaps that is true of most of us as we grow older and get the notion that somehow things were better in days gone by or as we sometimes say, "In the good old days," than they are in the troubled times we find ourselves in today. That may or may not be true, but it seems that when we were young, the problems belonged to those who were older and now that we are older, the problems belong to those who are younger. However that may be, my dreams often take me back to what I believe were simpler times.

I have often closed my eyes and visualized what the main street of my hometown was like the first time I walked down it as a young boy, nine years old. Those were the days when most store fronts were 25 feet wide, with fancy window displays and neon signs hanging over the sidewalk. All jewelry stores seemed to have large, free standing, double-faced clocks on the sidewalk out front and, as you walked, you had to dodge around the stairwells going down to barber shops and insurance offices located in the basements. That first day in town was a Sunday and, after church, we walked the two blocks to Wittimore's Rexall Drug Store to buy a Sunday paper. This drug store was on the corner and had one of those fancy soda fountains with the shiny marble counter and the long mirror on the back wall. In those days, the Sunday paper had the funnies on the outside and you could easily find the peach colored sports page. As we walked to the drug store, we first passed Quigg's Fairway Market, where I was to spend summers and after school hours working as a delivery boy when I was in high school. Next, we passed Dingman's Cleaners, the National Tea Food Store, and a photography studio located in a large white house set back from the street. This photography studio had a lighted case in front showcasing the talents of the photographer. Next came the J.C. Penney store, Secker's Grocery and the Rapids Theatre which was the home of the Saturday morning Cowboy Shows which set you back ten cents if you sat in the first twelve rows. Oh, how I enjoyed Gene Autry, Roy Rogers, Hopalong Cassidy, the Cisco Kid, the Lone Ranger and others, while sitting in one of those ten-cent seats. And what about their side-kicks such as Smiley Bennett, Fuzzy St. John and Tonto? As we left the theatre we passed Tayler's Buster Brown Shoe Store before we arrived at the drug store corner. Across the street, standing by itself in the center of a city block, was Central School where I would start third grade in a short time. The rest of Main Street continued for three more blocks, crossing the railroad tracks and culminating at the paper mill which sat on the banks of the Mississippi River.

They don't make main streets like that anymore. It was so wide that cars could park diagonally on both sides and down the center. Nothing that I have described in this first block remains, except for beautiful old Central School, now a museum with a few specialty shops. All else has changed just as I have. Oh, what fun it is to dream and reminisce!

Some Thoughts on Retirement

My decision to retire from full-time work when I reached age sixty-five was a decision made long ago-long before the time I would start counting the days to my sixty-fifth birthday. Having once made that decision, I never seriously considered changing it. There was no requirement that I retire at age sixty-five. In fact, I could continue until age seventy before I would be faced with mandatory retirement.

I have always believed that one should step down from a career while still having a relatively sharp edge for the work. As I have told my fellow judges of my retirement plans, many seemed surprised and questioned me as to why I was doing it. My reply was usually that I had been a judge long enough and wanted to step aside while I was young enough to enjoy life and do some things I had long dreamed of doing. I could not tell some of them that I had noticed over the years that those judges who stayed until they were seventy were often the ones who should have quit at sixty-five and those who quit at sixty-five were often the ones who should have stayed until seventy.

Shortly before I retired, as I sat alone in my Chambers waiting to be called on the phone for a newspaper interview, I tried to foresee what questions I would be asked and how best to answer them. I had the same experience again, a few days later as I waited for an interview by the editor of our local newspaper. I found both interviews to be very stimulating. Many questions were asked that I had not anticipated and that required a fair amount of thought before replying. The person doing the second interview wanted to make sure the interview took a different approach than the first one. The second interview was special to me because the person doing the interview was the new editor of the Litchfield Independent

Review. He grew up in Dawson, Minnesota and that is where I began my legal career in 1966. His parents are my very good friends and we have kept in touch- off and on- over the years. I remember the editor as a little boy and now here he was-this little boy-a grown man- asking me probing questions about my career, my family and my life. I thought how proud his parents would be if they could hide in my robe closet and listen in. When the interview was over we talked about his parents and his siblings and I listened with great interest as he told me what each of his brothers was now doing.

As we shook hands and said our good-byes after he had taken a couple of pictures, I thought- how fascinating. My career began in Dawson and here I am being interviewed by this young man who was a child there at the start of it and is now beginning his career as an editor in Litchfield as my career nears its end in this community!

Risks

I do not like to admit that I sometimes sit and daydream. I find this to be pleasurable, even though I was taught very young that dreaming was a waste of time and something to be avoided. I remember being told, "Only lazy people daydream." Well, one of the thoughts I seem to return to often in my dreams is "Why do so many people spend their entire life in one place?" I ask myself, is it the closeness of family or perhaps the fear of the unknown? Could it be the difficulty we have with making decisions and, before we know it we are entrenched? Or maybe the family business makes life too comfortable to consider leaving. My own conclusion is that we often fail to live out our dreams because of the risk involved. After all, risk-taking is not easy and the fear of failure is great. We often hear people say "Why did he do that - he must have known it would not work", or " I could have told him that would fail."

I look back on my life and remember all those times I would ask myself, "Where will I be ten years from now and what will I be doing?" I have those same thoughts now as I think about my life's journey. As I look back, I remember the risks I have taken. The risk of getting married and letting another person know who I am; the risk of moving out in the country to an unknown place to practice law in a smaller town than I had ever lived in before; the risk of running for election as a judge; the risks involved with raising a family in a world that seems to get more complicated and insecure with each passing year. But now those risks are behind me and I find myself dreaming of risks still to be taken or not. Do we stay where we are or do we move to a place where growing old is made a little easier? Do we move closer to my home where I have several siblings in the twilight of their lives? And then, remembering that the risk of getting married was a risk well taken, do we move closer to the Twin Cities to be near my wife's family?

Of course, I do not know what the future holds for us. Perhaps it makes sense to consider a move to a place not too far away where growing old would be made simpler and we would both be somewhat close to our roots. Whatever we do, I know for sure there will be risks involved.

Kate Weyrens

Writing is my way of reconciling my reflective, inner self, with my active, extroverted self. This has always been a challenge for me. The days of my retirement are a gift, which I am learning to use creatively as an act of being rather than an act of doing.

A Bonfire with Instruments

"Grammy and Granpa, we can't have a bonfire without instruments!" The campfire sputtered, hesitated and burst into a dance of indigo, red and blue which flashed against the shadows of the night. Morgan gathered her instruments from the camper. Kneeling, she set them around her, a tambourine, drum, and pipe. Quietly and confidently she picked up the tambourine. In the firelight, against the warm darkness of the September night sky, she began to sway back and forth to the rhythm of her own song, the tambourine a blur of movement in her hands. Her tiny four-year-old body, a kaleidoscope of shadows, dark and light, framed by the blackness of the ancient pines that surrounded the campsite. I followed the height of a pine with my eyes up to the small circle of nocturnal sky, sparkling with stars, that was defined by the tops of the pine branches. "The stars are in the water and the fire pushes through the cracks," she sang. As she finished with the tambourine, she picked up the pipe. The quiet was pierced by the rapid whistle of the pipe as she danced to her own rhythm. Finally, she took the small drum, sat on a log and as her head bobbed to the rhythm, she tapped the drum. Then it was Granpa's turn. His marveling and his love was reflected in his eyes. Who can describe the mystery of this kind of beauty? I am forever changed. My heart has expanded. This night helped me rediscover my own music. Then, as I began to dance and sing, all the inhibitions of being an adult dissolved in the velvety darkness and the intimacy of the moment. "The stars are in the water and the fire pushes through the cracks." The wonder is in my eyes and the mystery of this love pushes through the cracks in my heart.

The Hat

I feel bold, courageous, nuts and giddy when I wear The Hat. It is a dark, wheat-colored straw, with a high, rounded crown and a three-inch brim. A wide, orange grosgrain ribbon circles the crown. The piece de resistance is the large flower, with a yellow center, which stands tall on a green stem and waves its orange, somewhat iridescent feathers front and center above my face.

My Mother brought me The Hat as a gift from Arizona some thirty-five odd years ago. There is something of the lighthearted, mirthful person that snickered out of my Mom now and then that transforms my heart ever so slightly each time I look at The Hat. Through it I feel one with my Mom and one with myself. When she gave it to me, I had very young children and, once in a while, I golfed at the Dawson Golf Club on Ladies Day. And I always wore The Hat. "Laugh a little," it said to my friends. "Veg out!" it said to me.

It was part of a clown costume for anyone in the family for many years. And it has healing powers, just like my Mom did. It is said that laughter is healing. Many a time I have reached for it to take to a woman friend when I felt helpless before the unspeakable pain that filled her life. The Hat said: "We have shared precious moments of our lives. I want to share this with you, too. Laughter and tears are so close. Let this be a portent of your healing." Sometimes I have left it for many months-as when my friend, Mary, was going through chemo for breast cancer. Through it I said, "Hang on. Keep it all in perspective and, once in a while, put this hat on, look in the mirror and laugh a little."

When I gather with my women friends for a day or two to share our lives and our hearts, I love to arrive wearing The Hat.. It signals for me that I am on an R and R. And I love the joy it brings to other people. There is an ache in all of this too that is right there under the surface. I don't need to discuss it with myself or others midst our laughter. But there is a resolve that is heightened within me to use this as my spirit instructs me to, because, for my Mom, The Hat did two things: revealed her loving, playful heart and camouflaged her pain.

The Hat. Its just a silly, little gift from my Mom. And so is my life.

Thanks, Mom.

Bad Tölz

"We better load the car and get moving. Germany is beautiful but there is too much traffic and, since this is such a beautiful October Sunday, there will be lots of families heading to the mountains." Georg, my cousin Leni's husband, directed us as we prepared to leave their home in Munchen and head into the Bavarian Alps to Bad Tölz, the mountain village where Leni was born, the granddaughter of my dad's Uncle Hans. Leni and Georg were fluent in English and I was able to spit out the essentials in Deutsch.

The day unfolded before us as Leni and Georg were most generous with their hospitality and their plans for us but let us discover it as we went. Unbeknownst to us, we were embarking on a day that filled our cups to the fullest.

Leni and Georg are the parents of three: two teenagers, Heidi and Joseph and five-year-old Leonard. Initially, reluctant to try out the English they were learning in school, they quickly loosened up as they heard my struggling attempts to ask their ages: Vie alt sind Sie?" and especially when I told them auf Detsch that I was seventy-five rather than fifty-seven.

Soon we arrived in Bad Tölz at the home of Leni's seventy-eight year old Mother, also named Leni, Leni Kugler, which was my maiden name. Leni was ready for us and off we went to the foot of the Alps about five miles out of town. We pulled into the parking lot and there, before us, was a gondola, with lines of families waiting to buy tickets. "Where are they going I asked?" "Oh, they are waiting to go up the mountain. Families here often spend their Sundays hiking in the Alps," was the reply as we took our tickets and waited our turn to get into a gondola. And then we were off - eight of us - ages seventy-eight to five. The panorama before us was one of valleys, distant peaks, lush greenery and families, families out enjoying the magnificent beauty of the day and this incredible part of the world. The elder Leni led the way: "When you have spent your life in the mountains like I have, age is an advantage." Obviously that was true. Her sparkling eyes, her shortly cropped gray hair, her ready smile and ruddy complexion and her strong, sure gait supported her statement. From the end of the gondola, she led us to the top of the mountain, about a 1650 meter hike. Occasionally Leonard bounded ahead only to be swiftly and firmly corralled by his dad as another cliff came into view. The mountainside was dotted with short single file lines of families, following the paths up or down the mountainside. They were visible in every direction. What would it be like to be able to spend your Sundays like this, we wondered aloud. Our cousins smiled politely, and seemed sincerely flattered by our enthusiasm over the treasure that we had just discovered. Their quiet pleasure at our response indicated a confident, lifelong awareness and appreciation of this treasure that was indeed an important part of the Kugler heritage.

The day soon took on a surreal character for me. My senses were heightened, I was quietly but acutely aware of everyone and everything around me. I was aware also of an excitement deep in my soul which needed to be balanced by my calm demeanor so that I could indeed take in as much of this as possible. Underlying all of these feelings was the awareness that my own grandfather had left these roots at the age of thirteen because his mother had died, his father remarried and the new wife did not want him. Andrew, my grandpa, was the oldest and the family was miserably poor. He was sent to St. John's University at Collegeville, Minnesota, to be a priest - a course in life which obviously he changed. He carried a quiet sorrow and anger about him all of his life because he never saw any of his siblings again, and that included the elder Leni's father, my great uncle, Hans. And thus my father carried some of this pain, too. So for me, this was indeed a journey of re-connection and reconciliation. During the war Grandpa had sent money and packages to Deutschland. And here we were, close to the site of Dachau. The smoke from the furnaces had been visible from the streets of Bad Tölz. The German troops had taken over Uncle Hans' family home during the war and thus had ruined his furniture making business.

We walked the mountain paths from knoll to knoll. On these knolls were perched parasailers and hang gliders waiting their turns for the next flight. We stood transfixed as one after another of these brightly colored purple, red, green and yellow wings glided off the edge of the cliffs and sailed quietly over the wooded valleys of these Bavarian Alps. Every time I turned to look at Aunt Leni, as I called her, she was watching my reactions and smiling broadly. Aunt Leni spoke little English and yet the warmth and connection between us was tangible and intense. "Are you getting hungry?" questioned Georg as he pointed out one of the many Bavarian Gasthaus buildings that are scattered around the mountainside. And then we sat down to delicious brats, sauerkraut and Deutsch beer. In the late afternoon my cousins indicated that it was time to head back to the gondola. Leonard objected and said he was going to walk down the mountain. After some discussion it was decided that the elder Leni and Jack and myself would ride in the gondola, and the young family would walk down. As we floated over their heads in the gondola we watched Leonard skip and jump over the crevices and rocks, as the family held hands and raced us down the mountainside.

At this point Jack and I realized that we both were feeling that time had stood still and we knew that was a signal to us of the deep meaning of the hospitality that we were experiencing. We then returned to the small apartment building that Aunt Leni had owned for years. There was a camping store on the ground level which the family ran some years back. Then there were three apartments above, each occupying the entire floor that it was on. We spent about an hour in Aunt Leni's apartment watching the election returns on TV, since it was the day of general elections in Deutschland. Suddenly, Hilde, one of Aunt Leni's daughters, burst into the room. "We have a Bavarian feast ready for you. Please come up stairs to our apartment."

And there, in the living room, was an array the likes of which we had never seen. Hilde and Leni and their families were glowing with delight. "This is what we always serve when we have a truly Bavarian celebration," they chorused. Hilde had two teenagers and they with Leni and Georg's children had helped surprise us. There was a large, ornately carved wooden booth in the corner of the room. The table was covered with platters of meat, cheeses, bread and vegetables. Delicious Deutsch broth completed the array. Large steins of Deutsch beer were raised as they sang a toast.

We delighted in each other, in our connectedness, the depth of which neither Deutsch nor English could adequately describe. Lifetimes, wars, sorrows and joys blended into the healing created by the grand hospitality of my family. Finally, Georg said, "We'd better be going. There will be much traffic on the road." With warm embraces, promise of future contacts and invitations to come to America, we bade them "auf Wiedersehen!"